"I think of you a lot. And the baby."

Her curiosity got the best of her. "Do you?"

He faced her and, if it weren't hot enough already outside, her cheeks instantly heated beneath his intense scrutiny.

"In fact, I think about that night a lot."

"Hmm. The sex."

"Not the sex." He dipped his head. "Though, it was good. Mighty good."

"Cole, we can't." She moved away, putting some much-needed distance between them.

He stopped her with a gentle tug on her elbow. "What I think about is the talking. The holding. The sleeping in each other's arms and waking up together with you beside me. The smell of your hair and the softness of your skin."

Vi could feel her resistance slowly melting.

Dear Reader,

It's interesting how many changes a story can go through from its early stages to the finished book. *Having the Rancher's Baby* started out one way. When my editor read my original idea, she asked, "What if Cole was the father of Violet's baby?" and, like that, the story went in a whole new direction.

Having a baby when circumstances aren't ideal can be difficult. I tried hard to create realistic people in Cole and Violet. Showing their growing love for each other, and for their unborn baby, in the face of so many obstacles was a joy for me to write. I hope it's a joy for you to read.

I'm also pleased to announce that a portion of my royalties for this book is being donated to the wild horse sanctuary in Shingletown, California. If you have a moment, please check out the great work this organization does to protect the future of wild horses at wildhorsesanctuary.org. These amazing animals are truly living legends.

Warmest wishes,

Cathy McDavid

CathyMcDavid.com

Facebook.com/CathyMcDavid

Twitter.com/CathyMcDavid

HAVING THE RANCHER'S BABY

—

CATHY McDAVID

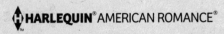

Recycling programs
for this product may
not exist in your area.

ISBN-13: 978-0-373-75621-6

Having the Rancher's Baby

Printed in U.S.A.

www.Harlequin.com

Since 2006, *New York Times* bestselling author **Cathy McDavid** has been happily penning contemporary Westerns for Harlequin. Every day, she gets to write about handsome cowboys riding the range or busting a bronc. It's a tough job, but she's willing to make the sacrifice. Cathy shares her Arizona home with her own real-life sweetheart and a trio of odd pets. Her grown twins have left to embark on lives of their own, and she couldn't be prouder of their accomplishments.

Books by Cathy McDavid

Harlequin American Romance

Mustang Valley

Last Chance Cowboy
Her Cowboy's Christmas Wish
Baby's First Homecoming
Cowboy for Keeps
Her Holiday Rancher
Come Home, Cowboy

Sweetheart, Nevada

The Rancher's Homecoming
His Christmas Sweetheart
Most Eligible Sheriff

Reckless, Arizona

More Than a Cowboy
Her Rodeo Man
The Bull Rider's Son

Visit the Author Profile page
at Harlequin.com for more titles.

Chapter One

"Easy does it, Hotshot."

Cole Dempsey nudged the paint gelding slowly forward. One step, two steps, then wait.

The six steers at the end of the corral shifted nervously and bunched closer together. Several ears twitched impatiently. Every pair of eyes stared unblinkingly. No one, not horse, rider or steer, moved for a full thirty seconds.

"See him?" Cole murmured. "Number 497."

As if in answer, Hotshot turned his head to the left, something horses did to bring an object into better focus. In this case, it was the steer with the white patch on his chest. The one getting ready to bolt.

Cole was pleased. What the horse lacked in experience he made up for with inherent cow sense. A few more months' training under his belt, and Hotshot would make a respectable, if not outstanding, cutting horse. Cole might even cross-train the horse for calf roping. Along with cow sense, both required speed, agility and fearlessness.

"Let's go!" He pushed Hotshot into a quick run at the small herd, which split at the center like pins being scattered by a bowling ball.

Number 497 took off, instinctively heading for the gate. Cole and Hotshot followed, matching the steer's every twist and turn as if attached by an invisible cord. Within seconds, they separated the steer from the rest of the herd and ran him to the far end of the corral. He reached the corner and turned to face them, awaiting his fate.

Cole pulled Hotshot to a stop. In a real team penning event, they would have herded the steer into a small holding pen, then gone after the next one until the required three were rounded up and contained. Today, they settled for simply boxing him in a corner.

"Good job." Cole reached down to give Hotshot a pat on the neck.

The horse had hardly broken a sweat, while Cole was drenched in it, his hair plastered beneath the tattered straw cowboy hat he wore. Mid-May, early afternoon, and the temperature was already in the high eighties. Southern Arizona tended to be like that, alternating between an oven and a boiler room six months of the year. Far different from northern California, where Cole grew up.

Some might say he hailed from here, Mustang Valley. Technically, they'd be right. But his mother had taken him and his older brother, Josh, away when Cole was five to live with their grandparents. California was and always would be home to him. Dos Estrellas, his late father's six-hundred-acre cattle ranch, now owned by him, Josh and their half brother, Gabe, was a temporary place for Cole to hang his hat. Nothing more.

As soon as the ranch was free of the debt incurred during their father's lengthy battle with colon cancer, and Cole's brothers purchased his share, he planned on returning to the rodeo circuit and his life as a professional cowboy.

In the meantime, he filled his days working as a wrangler and learning the cattle business, whether he wanted to or not. Whenever he found a free hour or two, he trained one of Josh's girlfriend's rehabilitated mustangs. Hotshot was the first to show potential for being more than a dime-a-dozen ranch horse. The first to light a fire in Cole, albeit a small one.

Practicing on green broke cutting horses wasn't the same as busting broncs or riding a bull, but team penning was a close cousin to rodeo and, for a while anyway, allowed Cole to be his old self.

"Get a move on." Waving his coiled lasso over his head, he walked Hotshot along the fence, encouraging number 497 to rejoin the others.

"You're sweating the fat clean off those steers."

Hearing a familiar voice, Cole turned in the saddle.

Violet Hathaway, ranch foreman and the only female on Dos Estrellas's payroll, strolled unhurriedly toward the corral, her boots stirring up dust with each step. She wore her usual attire, a worn blue work shirt and faded jeans. Nonetheless, she looked good. Too good for Cole to tear his gaze away. Not that he tried very hard.

Careful, pal, he warned himself. Thinking of her in those terms was a waste of energy. She was off-limits and had made that crystal clear.

She stopped at the railing. "Skinny steers won't bring in much money at the sale next month."

They'd had this discussion before. Every time he borrowed a few head for practice.

"What are you doing here on your day off?" he asked.

Sundays were usually quiet at the ranch. Barring an emergency, Violet always stayed home—home being a cozy house on the outskirts of town. Cole had recently learned that about the ranch foreman, along with a few more interesting tidbits, such as the fact that she owned two cats and read gossip magazines.

"Tying up a few loose ends." She grabbed the top railing and studied Hotshot with her expert eye. "He looks good."

"Thanks. Hard to believe he was near starving three months ago."

"Just goes to show you what regular meals and a little TLC will do."

The drought last winter had been hard on the few remaining wild mustangs in the area. Hotshot had belonged to a ragtag group rounded up near the Salt River and brought to the sanctuary on Dos Estrellas in the hopes that he might be fattened up and adopted out. Now he belonged to Cole.

He rode the horse over to Violet, offering a smile as he dismounted. Looping the reins around the saddle horn, he rested an arm on the top railing near her hand. He and Violet were face-to-face, except that he had a good five inches on her. She was forced to lift her chin in order to meet his gaze.

Truth be told, he liked her petite stature. She was a lot of snap, crackle and pop in one small package. A very attractive package.

"It's Sunday," he said. "The day of rest."

"Yeah, well, no rest for the wicked."

He let his voice drop and his eyes rove her face. "You're not wicked, Vi." Though she could be flirtatious and fun when she let loose.

For the briefest of seconds, she went still. Then— strange for her, as Violet usually oozed confidence— she turned away. "I asked you not to call me that."

"I like Vi. It suits you."

And it was personal. Something just the two of them shared. Calling her Vi was his way of reminding her about the night they'd spent together, which he supposed explained her displeasure. She didn't like being reminded.

She'd made the mistake of telling him that Vi was a childhood nickname, one she'd insisted on leaving behind upon entering her teens. They'd been alone, lying in bed and revealing their innermost feelings. Unfortunately, the shared intimacy hadn't lasted, disappearing with the first rays of morning sunlight.

"Cole." She sighed.

"What?" He feigned innocence.

"You know what. We agreed."

"To what? Me not calling you Vi?"

"Don't joke."

She was definitely out of sorts today. And pale. She hadn't been feeling well all week, which might account for her prickliness. Not that she'd complained to anyone, but he'd noticed.

"Okay." He shrugged one shoulder. "No joking."

Finally. A smile from her, though it was a small one. Even so, a powerful jolt shot through Cole. She really was lovely. Vivid green eyes, reddish-brown hair reaching well past her shoulders and twin dimples combined to give her an irresistible girl-next-door appeal.

No surprise she kept that bubbly personality under wraps. Otherwise, she'd be fighting the guys off right and left.

"I was wondering. If you weren't busy later…" She let the sentence drop.

"I'm not busy." Cole leaned closer, suddenly eager. "What do you have in mind?"

Could she have had a change of heart? They weren't supposed to see each other again socially or bring up their one moment of weakness. According to Vi, it had been a mistake. A rash action resulting from two shots of tequila each, a crowded dance floor and both of them weary of constantly fighting their personal demons.

Cole didn't necessarily agree. Sure, the road was not without obstacles. As one of the ranch owners, he was her boss. On the other hand, *she* oversaw *his* work while he learned the ropes. Confusing and awkward and a reason not to date.

But incredible lovemaking and easy conversation didn't happen between just any two people. He and Vi had something special, and he'd have liked to see where it went, obstacles be damned.

Strange, he hadn't given her a second thought before their "mistake." One moment on a dance floor and, boom, everything had changed. A shame she didn't feel the same.

Unless she did and was better at hiding it? The possibility warranted consideration.

"We need to, um, talk." She closed her eyes and, pressing a hand to her belly, swallowed with obvious difficulty.

"Hey, are you okay?"

"Yeah. Just this darn stomach flu."

He was becoming concerned. Her bout with the flu had been hanging on far too long. "Maybe you should see a doctor."

"Maybe." She squeezed her eyes shut, appearing to be fighting another wave of nausea.

"Are you sure you feel all right?"

"Yeah."

"Let me put Hotshot up. I'll return the steers later." They'd be fine for the time being, as there was both a metal shade covering and a water tank in the corral. "Give me ten minutes."

She nodded, and he led the horse to the gate, expecting her to be standing there. By the time he opened the latch, however, Vi was gone. He caught sight of her running across the open area toward the horse stables.

Cole frowned. She was certainly in a hurry. A big hurry.

He walked toward the stables, Hotshot following along.

The closer he got, the more his concern mounted. She was normally healthy as a, well, as a horse.

Entering the stables, he started down the aisle. Where had she gone? There weren't many places to choose from. He settled on the tack room as the most logical one. If she wasn't there, he could at least tether Hotshot to the post outside the door while he searched elsewhere.

Horses nickered as they went by, some of them stretching their long necks for a sniff or a nip at Hotshot's hind quarters. He took the attention in stride, displaying yet another good quality.

Cole tied Hotshot to the post and opened the tack room door. It was dark inside, and no one answered when he called out. Maybe Vi had headed to the house. He started back down the aisle, only to stop short at the sound of retching and choking.

"Vi? Is that you?"

He followed the sound three stalls down to the only empty one in the entire stables. Vi was there, bent at the waist, her long hair forming a silky curtain that shielded her face.

"Whoa. Are you okay?"

She coughed and held out a hand as if to ward him off. "Leave me alone."

Like hell he would. Cole strode forward and reached her just as her knees buckled and she slumped to the ground.

This wasn't how Violet had wanted to start her conversation with Cole, the two of them crammed elbow to elbow in the restroom behind the stables.

He ran the cold water in the tiny sink, wet a paper towel and handed it to her. "Here. You missed a spot." He motioned to her face.

"I did?" She automatically touched her chin and cringed.

Yep, there it was. She quickly wiped her entire face on the chance she'd missed another blob, then tossed the paper towel in the wastebasket. "Sorry."

"Nothing I haven't seen before."

She wondered about that. How many times, exactly, had he seen a woman lose her lunch before collapsing in his arms? Did he make a habit of hurrying them to the nearest bathroom and dispensing wet paper towels? Apparently so, because he was fairly adept at it.

"You don't say." She tried not to sound curious.

"On the circuit. There's always one guy who upchucks after finishing his run."

Riding a bucking bull or horse. Being tossed through the air and landing hard. That would definitely be a reason to throw up.

She reached for the doorknob, utterly humiliated and more than ready to leave.

He waylaid her with a hand on her arm. "Are you sure you're all right?"

"I'm fine."

"You don't seem fine to me."

"I'm probably dehydrated." Violet knew that wasn't the case, but no way was she telling Cole what ailed her. Not while she wore a vomit-stained shirt and her queasy stomach threatened to revolt again any minute.

Shouldering open the bathroom door, she stepped outside and gulped fresh air like a miner newly released after days in an underground tunnel.

"I'll take you to the clinic if you want."

Cole stood beside her. *Right* beside her. She told herself she was being overly sensitive and that he *wasn't* looking her up and down with far too much curiosity.

"Thanks, but you don't have to do that."

"I don't mind."

Mustang Valley's one small urgent-care center was open most days. Violet doubted the nurse on duty could do anything for her that she hadn't done already.

Rubbing her forehead, she inhaled slowly. The air might be fresh, but the sun was hot and stifling. "You don't have to take me, because I'm not going."

"Vi, be reasonable. You're sick."

"I asked you not to call me that," she snapped, then gritted her teeth. "Sorry." She was apologizing a lot today and would again if they continued this conversation.

"You're right," he said. "I shouldn't tease you when you're not feeling well."

Did he always have to be so nice to her? Violet suspected he showed her a side of himself he kept from most people. The night they'd spent together was an example of that. He'd been funny and sweet in the bar when they were dancing, attentive and passionate when they'd made love and tender when he'd cradled her in the aftermath.

Were he not Cole Dempsey, they'd probably be dating now. Perhaps optimistic about what the future held for them.

Yet he *was* Cole Dempsey and wrong for her for too many reasons to list. Not only was he her boss, which in itself was bad enough, but he'd been adamant from the day he arrived that he had no intention of remaining in Mustang Valley. Violet didn't blame him; she might feel similarly in the same circumstances. But she needed someone who was willing to put down roots.

She certainly wasn't traipsing after a man whose only interest was the next town and the next rodeo. Not in her condition. Not any time, ever.

Would Cole insist on staying when she told him? Violet had no expectations. The only reason she'd considered saying anything today was because she couldn't hide her pregnancy much longer. This morning sickness—correction, *all-day* sickness—was kicking her in the butt and difficult to explain away.

That was new, but not the other symptoms. She'd been pregnant three times previously, back when she was married. She'd miscarried all three times, never making it past week seven. Until now.

She was over eight weeks along. There was no question as to the date of conception or the father's identity. She'd broken her celibacy streak only once in the past three years, and that was with Cole.

Pregnant from a one-night stand? No one was going to believe her. She hardly believed it herself.

"What are you thinking?" he asked, interrupting her thoughts and returning her to the present.

"That I shouldn't have eaten chicken salad for lunch."

She started for her truck, parked near the stables, deciding she'd been wrong to approach Cole today. Better to wait until her second trimester. With her history, the odds of carrying to term weren't in her favor.

A painful lump promptly formed in Violet's throat. She wanted this baby with the same intensity she'd wanted all the others. After the last miscarriage, and her marriage falling apart, she'd given up the dream of ever having a big, happy family.

Then, suddenly, she'd been thrown a crumb. A tiny positive sign on the early pregnancy testing wand and a second one a week later, just to be sure.

Could fate be playing another cruel trick on her, or was it answering her prayers at last?

Another wave of nausea struck. Violet reminded herself it was a good sign. The more numerous her symptoms, the stronger they were, the better chance the fetus was thriving. Not like before.

"Are you going home?" Cole asked.

Honestly, could he be any harder to shake loose? "Yes. See you tomorrow." Her truck was only a few feet away.

He kept pace with her, and she groaned softly. Apparently, she needed to be blunt. Tell him straight out to beat it.

"I can follow you home," he said. "In case you feel dizzy again."

She stuffed her hand in her side pocket, searching for her keys. Finding them, she wiped her damp brow. Sweet heaven, it was warm today. "No, you need to put Hotshot away and return those steers to the pasture."

"Is that an order?" A hint of amusement colored his voice.

If her stomach wasn't busy trying to empty itself, she might have found his remark funny. As it was, she desperately needed to get away before she lost whatever small amount of her lunch remained.

"Now that you mention it." She tried to smile. All she accomplished was a trembling of her lower lip.

"Vi, let me help you."

He sounded sincere and well-intentioned. If only he weren't waiting for the day when he could hit the road.

"I'm fine."

She might have maintained her composure if he hadn't reached for her hand and linked their fingers. She'd always been a sucker for a man who held hands. It was so intimate and personal. Her grandparents had been like that, holding hands until the day Papa Hathaway passed away.

A soft sob broke free, and Violet pressed a fist to her mouth. Besides being sick every waking hour, she was also fast becoming an emotional wreck, crying at the least little thing.

Hormones, she reminded herself. Manufacturing lots of them was another sign that her pregnancy was progressing. Still, hormones were nothing but trouble when facing her baby's father and not wanting to tell him in case the worst happened.

"What's wrong?" he asked, his startling blue eyes filled with concern.

She'd lost herself in those eyes before.

"I'm just tired." It was true. She slept more than ever, yet struggled to stay awake during the day. "Think I'll go home and take a nap."

When she would have opened her truck door, he held fast to her hand, waylaying her. "Don't take this the wrong way…"

Uh-oh. She suddenly tensed, not liking his tone. "Cole, please. Let me go." When he didn't, every nerve in her body went on high alert. "Please," she repeated.

He hesitated, his thumb caressing the back of her hand, then blurted, "Vi, are you by any chance…pregnant?"

No! He couldn't have guessed. How could he? Men weren't that astute. Especially single, childless ones.

Panicking, she brushed him aside. "Why would you even think that?"

"I bunked with a friend and his wife for a few months last summer. She was pregnant. Had a lot of the same stuff wrong with her that you do. Tired. Throwing up. Dizzy. Moody."

"Moody!"

He outright laughed. "It wasn't an insult."

"Glad you find me so funny." She concentrated on trying to hold down the contents of her stomach. "And, in answer to your accusation, don't be silly."

"No reason to get defensive." He released her hand, only to tuck a stray lock of hair behind her ear. His touch was gentle and, there was no mistaking it, affectionate. "If you were pregnant, we'd need to make some decisions."

He assumed he was the father. She didn't know whether to be appalled at his arrogance or flattered that he took for granted she didn't go to bed with just anyone and at the drop of a hat.

"It's hot." Sweat pooled between her breasts. "I need to get out of the sun."

"Let's go to the ranch house. No one's home till suppertime."

She shook her head, which only exacerbated her nausea. "We have nothing to talk about." Yet.

He stepped closer. "You're saying there's no chance you're pregnant?"

Her reply was to double over and throw up on his boots.

Chapter Two

Cole set a paper plate with a slice of dry toast in front of Vi. "Here you go."

"You don't have to do this."

She watched him intently as he slid in beside her at the kitchen table. Despite her earlier protests, he'd convinced her to accompany him to the ranch house.

"Eat up before it gets cold."

She did as he told her, delicately nibbling on a corner of the toast and following it with a sip of herbal tea.

"Have you decided what to do?" The question was foremost on his mind. Her answer would dictate the course of their conversation and, possibly, impact the rest of their lives.

"Thank you," she said quietly.

"For what?"

"Not asking if I was sure the baby's yours."

"We've worked together awhile now. I know you're a person of integrity and would tell me if I wasn't the father."

She nodded, examining the toast before taking another bite.

"Too done for you?" he asked.

"It's perfect."

"I pride myself on my toast. That and heating canned soup are my specialties." He offered her a grin.

She sighed. So much for his stab at humor.

"Fortunately for me," he continued, "Raquel's a wizard in the kitchen. If not, I'd starve."

At the mention of his late father's longtime companion, Vi become even more quiet. Cole didn't ask why. The Dempsey family dynamics were unusual to say the least and gave him his own share of somber moments.

Odd as it might seem, Cole liked Raquel, though he had plenty of reasons not to. She'd been his father's mistress for over thirty years, living with him the last twenty-five. She was also the reason Cole's father had cheated on, then divorced, his mother. The reason he'd ignored his two legitimate sons for most of their lives in favor of their half brother.

But Raquel was kind to Cole and Josh and doted on Josh's two children, whom she regularly babysat. She insisted on cooking big breakfasts and dinners every day, which the entire family shared, sparing Cole from relying on his own pathetic culinary skills.

She also wasn't responsible for his father's actions. August Dempsey had made his own choices. At any time, he could have reached out to his sons and included them in his life. As far as Cole was concerned, the blame lay entirely with his father.

It had been six months since he and Josh had returned to Dos Estrellas, and they were still struggling to find their places. Josh was doing a better job of fitting in than Cole, undoubtedly because he'd met and fallen in love with Cara, a family friend of Raquel's.

He also didn't resent their father to the degree Cole did. Josh's heart was unencumbered and free to love. Cole's was weighed down and locked tight.

Vi finished her toast and propped an elbow on the table. "What's wrong?"

"Nothing. Everything." She let her hands drop to her lap. "I think Raquel might have figured out I'm pregnant."

"She's pretty observant."

"So are you, apparently."

"Not really."

"You guessed easily enough."

"Well, about that." At her raised brows, he admitted, "I wasn't entirely honest with you earlier."

"You don't have a friend whose wife was pregnant?"

"That part's true. He's a good friend of mine." Cole shifted. "There was this other pregnant woman."

Vi stared at him pointedly. "My, you get around."

He immediately regretted opening his mouth. She might not appreciate this story. "It was a long time ago and doesn't matter."

"Then why not tell me?"

Talk had flowed easily between them the night they'd spent together. He'd revealed things about himself only his brother knew. How Cole's anger at his father, and his mother's bitterness, had tainted his entire life, prompting him to leave at eighteen and pursue a career in rodeo. The hardships endured during his years on the circuit. The rewards, which were few and far between.

Opening up to her now shouldn't be so difficult. Yet it was. That night, Vi hadn't been pregnant with his child. She'd been a woman he was attracted to and wanted to become better acquainted with. A woman he genuinely liked.

And because he liked and respected her, he supposed he owed her the truth about the kind of man she'd gotten herself tangled up with.

"I once dated a woman who was pregnant."

Violet gasped softly. "You have a child?"

"No." He shook his head. "She said the baby was mine, and I believed her. After about two months, I found out she was lying." It happened when he'd almost reconciled himself to the prospect of becoming a father. "Another cowboy was the dad. Seems when he left her high and dry, she went after me. I'd asked her out a few times before, which I suppose made me an easy target."

"How did you find out?"

"Josh and I were competing at the Frontier Days Rodeo, and one of my buddies clued me in. I told Josh, and he insisted I have a DNA test done before I committed to anything. When I suggested the test, she was furious at first, then came clean."

"What happened to her and the baby?"

"I saw her only once after we broke up. It was a few months later. She was with another cowboy. Not the baby's father," he added.

"Did you talk to him?"

"Naw. I just walked away. Figured it wasn't any of my business."

"Weren't you angry at her for lying?"

"Heck, yeah, I was angry. She told a huge lie. One that was unfair to both me and the baby."

"She must have been desperate."

"That doesn't make what she did right."

"Of course not."

"For the record, I'm not angry anymore." But he hadn't walked away from the relationship unscathed. In the nine years since, he'd yet to have a committed relationship. "Really, she dodged a bullet. I was twenty-one at the time and constantly broke. Hardly ready for a family or capable of supporting one."

He doubted he was better father material now. It wasn't just his occupation—a life on the road tended to be hard on loved ones. He was simply too much like August Dempsey. Selfish and unreliable.

"Are you or Josh going to insist I take a DNA test?" Vi asked.

Cole hesitated. This was a tricky question. He had every right to request the test, and it made good sense, considering what had happened in his previous relationship.

"Let me save you the trouble," she responded before he could. "I have no problem taking the test as soon as it's feasible."

"Okay." He leaned back in his chair. "Then I guess we can skip it."

"We'll see." She lifted her chin.

She had a lot of backbone, not that he'd thought differently. It was one of the qualities he'd liked about her from the day they'd first met, right here in this kitchen, in fact.

"How about this? I'll let you decide."

"Aren't you accommodating," she answered flatly.

"Cut me some slack, will you, Vi?" Cole had his faults. Beating around the bush wasn't one of them. "You've had, what, a month to get used to the idea? I've had maybe thirty minutes. The fact is, I'm not sure how I feel, what I think or what we should do. I need a little time. I don't think that's too much to ask."

He immediately regretted his small outburst.

Vi, however, reacted with reason. "Fair enough."

"I can tell you that I'll take responsibility for the baby. Pay you support."

"All right."

Was she mad? It was hard to tell.

Cole opened his mouth to defend himself, then promptly shut it. God, he sounded just like his father. Not his words so much. Cole remembered very little about his life at Dos Estrellas before his parents divorced. Rather, it was his attitude. August Dempsey had believed paying child support was plenty enough to do right by his sons.

"Are you planning on staying in Mustang Valley?" she asked.

"I rodeo for a living. I have to travel."

"You aren't now."

"I'm not making any money, either. I need an income." The ranch couldn't afford to pay any of the brothers a salary. Not while the bills owed totaled more than the revenue. He and his brothers withdrew only enough funds to cover their living expenses, and Cole's personal savings were almost depleted. "But I'll return as often as possible. Every few months at least. And be here when the baby's born."

Vi turned her head as if she, too, were biting her tongue.

Was visiting every few months too infrequent? Cole had no idea of what a reasonable schedule might be. His father hadn't made one trip to California and never offered for his sons to visit him. Every few months seemed like a lot in comparison.

A thought suddenly occurred to him. Vi might be expecting him to propose. Should he, or would that be rushing headlong into disaster?

"Can we wait a little while before deciding on the specifics?"

"Actually," she said, "I agree with you. Another month at least. But not for the reason you think." She paused. "I was married before. A long time ago."

"No fooling!"

"Is that so hard to believe?"

"No. Heck, no," he added for emphasis. "You just never said anything." Neither had Gabe or Raquel, not that Cole had inquired. "Were you married long?"

"Three years."

"You must have been young." She was only twenty-eight now. Three years of marriage plus "a long time ago" equaled early twenties by his calculations.

"I was. Young and idealistic and convinced we'd be happy the rest of our lives."

"What happened?"

Cole discovered he was interested. Very interested. While they'd lain wrapped in each other's arms, she'd told him about her first crush and having her heart broken in high school. Not one single peep about a husband. Ex-husband, he amended.

"Denny was a real sweetheart," she said. "Our breakup wasn't his fault. It wasn't mine, either. We simply weren't equipped to deal with the…problems we faced." Her voice cracked. "Some people never are, regardless of their age or how much they love each other."

Cole was tempted to take her hand again or run his fingertips along the curve of her cheek. He didn't, not sure she'd welcome the gesture.

"I got pregnant and lost the baby. Then it happened twice more." She sniffled. "Denny tried his best to give me what I needed. Love. Support. Encouragement. But it just wasn't enough—my grief overwhelmed us both. When I finally recovered, it was too late for us. I'd lost him, too."

"That must have been tough." Cole hoped Vi saw past his lame response and realized how sorry he felt for her and her then-young husband. "No one should have to go through that."

"I'm afraid of miscarrying again." Her teary gaze met his. "Very afraid."

Oh, the hell with it, he thought, and reached for her hand. "Who wouldn't be, in your shoes?"

She didn't pull away and, instead, squeezed his fingers. "I'm also afraid of losing what's important to me again. That was the hardest part."

Was she talking about him and their fledgling relationship? Apparently not, for she straightened and gently withdrew her hand from his.

"I have a doctor's appointment tomorrow. I should know more then."

"What time?"

"After lunch. Why?"

"Let me drive you."

Her eyes widened. "There's no need."

"I'm the baby's father."

"And you didn't bargain on that. I should have told you I wasn't using birth control."

"I shouldn't have assumed and taken precautions."

"Cole."

"Vi, let me go with you."

"Because it's the responsible thing to do?"

"Because I want to."

"People are going to ask questions or make assumptions. Especially Raquel. I'm not ready for that."

"We'll come up with a cover story. Stick with the stomach flu and say you're too dizzy to drive yourself."

After a moment, she relented. "Okay, you win."

"This isn't a contest."

"Sorry. I'm still getting used to this, too."

He smiled. "That offer to follow you home still holds."

"I'm better now," she insisted. "Why don't you return those steers to the pasture?"

He decided to follow her, anyway.

They left the ranch house by the kitchen door and walked to the horse stables, where Vi had parked her truck.

Before they parted, he said, "Call or text me later to let me know you're okay. Humor me," he added, when she started to object.

True, Cole was still grappling with impending fatherhood, but he had no doubts of his fondness for Vi or his concern for her well-being. He'd also bet money she harbored a similar fondness for him.

With luck, it might be enough to get them through the coming months, or possibly years.

VIOLET PASSED THE clipboard holding her completed medical forms over the counter to the receptionist, along with the pen she'd used.

"Do you have your insurance card?" the woman asked, more efficient than pleasant. She accepted the card Violet gave her and made a copy before returning it.

"You have a thirty-dollar co-pay," the receptionist informed her. Once the transaction was complete, she said, "Go ahead and take a seat. We'll call you when we're ready."

Violet didn't ask how long that might be. She'd been seeing Dr. Medina for eight years, long before her first pregnancy. In all that time, nothing in the office had changed. Not the neutral decor, not the generic furniture and definitely not the long wait times. Even the vase of silk flowers on the reception counter was the same.

On second thought, there was one big difference, and he sat in the corner, cowboy hat balanced on his lap. Every few seconds, one of the other two noticeably pregnant patients cast him a glance. An admiring one.

Understandable, Violet supposed. Cole had cleaned up for the appointment, donning what appeared to be a fairly new Western-cut shirt and his best jeans. He looked… handsome. She could admit that. Much the same as he'd looked that night in the Poco Dinero Bar when he'd sauntered over and joined her at the table she shared with her friends, the local grain supply rep and his wife.

Heaving a sigh, Vi plunked down in the chair beside Cole and propped her purse in front of her. If she was hoping to use it as a shield, she'd need something a lot bigger. A thick panel, maybe. Or simply distance.

She could quite literally *feel* him. Violet wasn't a romantic and, thanks to her parents' three-decades-long miserable marriage, she didn't subscribe to the theory of soul mates. But there was something about Cole that caused her to be acutely aware whenever he was in the same room. The sensation intensified when they were close and, she was certain of it, accounted for her weakness that night in the bar.

He was a competent dancer. Quite good, actually. She hadn't expected him to smoothly glide her across the crowded dance floor. Neither had she expected her insides to melt when he held her tight during the slow numbers.

She'd been prepared for nothing more intimate than a good-night hug in the parking lot at the end of the evening, but Cole had had other ideas and pulled her into his arms for a kiss.

An *amazing* kiss. Surprised at first, she'd quickly surrendered. Apparently, she'd invited him home, because the next thing she knew, they were both in the backseat of her friends' SUV, the lights of town passing by in a blur.

It was while she'd driven him to his truck the next morning that they'd talked and mutually agreed to forget what had happened.

Wait a minute. That wasn't quite accurate. She'd done all the talking. Cole had gone along with her without adding much to the conversation.

"Everything okay?" he suddenly asked.

"Just waiting my turn."

"How much was the co-pay? I'll reimburse you."

At least he had the decency to speak in a low voice. "Can we talk about this later?"

"I'm paying," he answered, his tone implying there'd be no further discussion.

She stood up, strode over to the periodical rack and grabbed a magazine on pregnancy. Years ago, she'd subscribed to this same one and had saved the back issues, storing them in a credenza drawer. After the third miscarriage, she'd burned every copy in her backyard fire pit.

Returning to her chair, she began flipping the magazine pages, barely noticing the ads and articles.

What had she been thinking, agreeing to let Cole accompany her? She was tired; that must be it. And sick. She'd been in no physical condition to put up a fight. Though today she actually felt pretty good and had managed not to lose her breakfast or her lunch.

She sneaked a glance at him, certain he had nothing whatsoever to do with her improved health.

"Would you like me to come with you?" he asked.

"Into the exam room?" She drew back in alarm. "Absolutely not."

He tensed.

All right, she'd overreacted. But if the doctor delivered bad news, and that was a distinct possibility, Violet didn't want Cole there to witness her emotional breakdown.

What if the doctor delivered good news? She was two months along, after all. Well, then she'd relay the information to Cole and they'd continue as they'd previously decided, not telling anyone until she reached her second trimester.

Even then, she'd insist on informing only close family and friends. Violet refused to take chances. Most people, though kind and well-intentioned, didn't have a clue about what she was going through. Their sympathy when she'd miscarried had worsened her grief rather than relieved it.

"Perhaps another time," she offered by way of apology.

"*Next* time," he countered.

His response thoroughly rattled her.

A quick check confirmed the one remaining patient was occupied with her phone and not paying them any attention.

"I thought you said you haven't figured out what to do yet. But you're planning to come with me to every appointment?"

He bent his head close to hers and spoke softly, yet deliberately. "I'm concerned about you and your health."

"Pardon me, but I'm confused."

"Not to steal your words, but can we talk about this later?"

"Fine." She went back to reading the magazine.

They waited another fifteen minutes when a nurse finally appeared in the doorway leading to the exam rooms. "Ms. Hathaway? This way, please."

Violet stood and would have gone if not for a gentle tug on her hand. It was Cole.

"Good luck."

Her insides melted, just as they had on the dance floor. For a moment, she wished he was concerned about more than her health. Enough to reconsider his plans of returning to the rodeo circuit.

He continued to occupy her thoughts as she walked down the corridor, throughout her weigh-in and blood pressure reading and when the nurse left her alone to change into the paper gown.

What kind of father would Cole make? He wasn't always caustic and abrupt. When he wanted, he had the ability to be sweet and tender and so very charming. She'd been the recipient of those qualities before and had basked in them.

If only their circumstances were different. What then?

Dating? Moving in together? Getting married? Violet wasn't sure she wanted any of that. They really didn't know each other well.

Once under way, the exam progressed quickly. Violet found herself watching and listening intently to Dr. Medina for even the tiniest indication that something might be wrong. There was none. The other woman remained chipper throughout the exam, telling Violet that all was well and exactly as it should be.

"Ready for a peek at your baby?"

Her words startled Violet, and she almost refused "Yes. I am."

"Because your pregnancy is high risk, we'll be doing a transvaginal ultrasound today." When the probe was in place, Dr. Medina pointed to the monitor screen at Violet's right. "There's your baby."

She adjusted the volume, and Violet heard a rapid beat matching the small pulsating heart visible in the middle of the fetus. All at once, she started to cry, unable to stop herself. She hadn't been far enough along during her other pregnancies to hear or see the heartbeat.

Dr. Medina smiled sweetly and handed Violet a tissue, her curly silver hair framing her face like a wreath. "Try not to worry too much. It won't do you or the baby any good."

Violet wiped at her tears. "It's hard not to worry."

"I'd like to see you in two weeks."

Immediately, Violet feared the worst. "Is something wrong?"

"Not at all. Just a precaution." Dr. Medina returned the probe to its holder. Next, she pressed a series of buttons on the ultrasound machine and printed a picture, which she gave to Violet. "Next month, when the baby's bigger, I'll send you to the imaging center for a more comprehensive ultrasound. They'll make you a CD."

Violet clutched the picture to her chest. She liked the sound of "next month."

Dr. Medina helped her to a sitting position, her hand remaining on Violet's shoulder to comfort her. "Call me if you have even the slightest cramping."

"All right." Violet had already programed the doctor's number into her phone's speed dial.

"Remind me again—you work at a cattle ranch, right?"

"Yes."

"Outdoors?"

"Almost always."

"And very physical."

"Comes with the territory." There'd been times when the demands of her job had been an escape for Violet. A cure for her various woes. Miscarriages. Failed marriage. Parents always arguing and trying to coerce her into choosing sides.

"I'm recommending you take it easy," Dr. Medina said. "Rest every day, and by rest I mean lying down, for at least two to three hours. Absolutely no lifting and no strenuous activities. That includes horseback riding."

Violet instinctively pressed a hand to her belly. She'd do nothing that might harm this baby. "I'll talk to my boss. Bosses. I have some vacation time coming. Maybe I can work something out."

"Sitting at a desk is fine, and I encourage you to walk. Exercise is beneficial as long as you don't go overboard."

They talked awhile longer about diet and prenatal vitamins and various dos and don'ts, most of which Violet already knew. Dr. Medina didn't mention the baby's father, though she was aware of Violet's divorce.

Violet bit back the urge to inquire whether having a

different father would improve her chances. They'd never figured out the cause of her miscarriages. Perhaps it had been genetic.

"See you in two weeks." Dr. Medina closed the door behind her when she left.

Violet took a moment to say a quiet prayer of thanks before climbing off the table and getting dressed. Her legs wobbled and her knees shook, as much from relief as nerves. In the waiting room, Cole glanced up when she entered, then stood nearby while she scheduled her next appointment with the receptionist.

"Do you need a reminder card?"

"Yes, thank you."

The woman completed the card and handed it to Violet, her eyes on Cole and filled with questions. She'd worked there for years and probably remembered Denny.

Violet tensed. It wasn't anyone's business who came with her to her appointments.

Cole didn't bring up her exam until they were on the road. "How did it go?"

She proceeded to tell him the basic details, but to her horror, started crying again when she got to the part about the ultrasound.

Cole reached across the console and took her hand. "I bet that was pretty neat to see."

Damn. Why did he have to be so nice?

"I have a picture. I'll make you a copy." She felt another sob coming on and countered it with a change in subject. "I need to set up a meeting with you and your brothers. As soon as possible. It's about my job."

Chapter Three

Cole pressed on the clutch and manually shifted the tractor into second gear. It was a John Deere, circa 1990, and groaned like a grumpy old man before the wheels finally gained traction. Hooked behind the tractor was a flatbed trailer loaded with hay. Cole turned the steering wheel hard to the right and chugged in the direction of the horse stables.

He was in charge of today's afternoon feeding. The job normally fell to one of the hands, but they were working with a skeleton crew today, in part because of Vi's absence. She'd taken off early to rest—something only Cole knew about—and to prepare for their five-thirty meeting.

She'd requested to speak with all three brothers. Again, Cole alone knew her reasons. She planned to tell them about her pregnancy and then request a modified work week that included fewer hours and light duty.

The meeting was scheduled for the only time Josh and Gabe were available—right before dinner. Nowadays, the demands on both men were many, and they were frequently gone from the ranch.

Josh had full custody of his two children while their mother, fresh from a sixty-day stint in drug rehab, proved her ability to remain sober. He and his girlfriend, Cara, were in the market for a new house and went out looking every chance they got. Cole expected the two of them to announce their engagement any minute, which was fine by him. He liked Cara. She made Josh happy and loved his children.

Gabe, too, was working his tail off. He divided his days between Dos Estrellas and their nearest neighbors, the Small Change Ranch. There, he helped his fiancée's Parkinson's-stricken father manage their large cattle operation. Gabe would be moving to the Small Change soon and assuming even more responsibilities. His marriage to Reese was scheduled to take place this spring, and they were already steeped in preparations.

Cole did his best to help out, filling in for both brothers when and where he could. Though he was a poor substitute for Raquel, he even babysat his niece and nephew on occasion.

Speak of the devil!

Rounding the corner, Cole caught sight of his three-year-old nephew not thirty feet in front of him, and hit the brakes hard. Dirt rose in a cloud as the tires skidded to a stop, and the heavily loaded flatbed trailer lurched, threatening to jackknife.

"What the…" Cole pushed his hat back and wiped his damp brow.

The boy walked alone, leading a small horse named Hurry Up. Like Hotshot, the mustang was a rehabilitated rescue from Cara's sanctuary. Tagging after them was a five-month-old Australian shepherd pup, a recent addition to the Dempsey household.

Cole cut the tractor engine, climbed down and jogged over to his nephew. "Hey, cowboy. What are you doing?"

Nathan stopped to gaze up at him. "Hi, Uncle Cole." He'd recently celebrated a birthday and since then had been talking up a storm, his vocabulary expanding daily. "I walking Hurry Up."

The horse and pup dutifully waited, the horse sniffing the dry ground, the pup chewing on a bent stick. Cole and Josh had once owned a horse and pup like these two when they were young. In Cole's opinion, there were no better playmates.

Hold on a minute. When did he start having opinions about kids' playmates? Maybe since he'd found out he might be a parent soon.

"Where's your dad?" he asked.

"Dunno."

Cole glanced around, not spotting his brother anywhere. Had Nathan wandered off? It wouldn't be the first time. The boy was mischievous with a capital *M*, a quality he definitely inherited from his father's side of the family. Both Josh and Cole had been notorious troublemakers in their day.

What if he had a son? Would the boy be a Dempsey through and through or more like Vi? Come to think of it, she'd probably been a bit of a troublemaker, too.

Perhaps the better question was what kind of father would Cole be? His few times babysitting hardly qualified him.

He could no doubt learn a lot from his older brother. Josh hadn't started out as the best of dads. Like Cole, he'd been a professional cowboy and away more than he was home. But after gaining sole custody of his two kids, Josh had stepped up, filling the role of single parent as if born to it.

Cole patted Nathan on the head. The boy wore a tattered cowboy hat not unlike his own, though Cole's fit better. "I think we should find your dad."

Nathan insisted on leading Hurry Up. They got about

fifty feet before Josh came running out of the horse stable, his year-old daughter, Kimberly, bouncing in his arms, his expression panicked. Spotting them, he drew up short.

Cole could see his brother struggling not to curse. He also saw the intense relief coursing through him. "Nathan! Criminy, son. How many times have I told you not to walk off like that?"

Nathan didn't appear the least bit remorseful. "Hi, Daddy. I walking Hurry Up."

The pup, thinking it was playtime, loped awkwardly over to Josh on gangly legs, the stick clenched in its mouth.

Cole waited for his brother to catch up. As they neared, his pretty little niece reached out her arms and babbled unintelligibly.

"You mind?" Josh handed over his daughter before Cole had a chance to reply.

"Hello, gorgeous." Cole balanced the little girl against his chest as he'd seen Josh do.

She babbled some more and patted his cheeks. It was cute. Maybe he wouldn't mind having a daughter.

Josh went down on one knee in front of his son. "Nathan, you can't leave without telling me. Do you understand?"

Nathan stared at his father, then slowly nodded. Cole suspected the boy didn't understand at all and was simply placating his dad.

Cole kept his niece busy and let father and son talk for several minutes. Eventually, Josh stood, emitting a long, low groan of frustration. "Kids," he said, as if that explained everything.

Before today, Cole might have answered, "I wouldn't know." Now, he kept his mouth shut.

After lifting Nathan onto the horse's back, Josh took Kimberly from Cole and plunked her in front of her brother. The two often went for rides, though lately Nathan had been less inclined to share, wanting Hurry Up for himself.

Josh gathered the lead rope in his hands. "What do you think the meeting's about today?"

"Guess we'll find out."

"Gabe figures she's going to ask for some time off, what with her parents divorcing."

"He could be right."

Josh studied Cole intently. "You know."

"Why do you say that?" Now would probably be a good time to return to feeding.

"You're hedging. You don't hedge."

"I promised Vi I wouldn't say anything. Violet," he quickly amended. Using a nickname implied intimacy.

His brother wasn't fooled. "You two have gotten friendly lately."

"We get along."

"Get along or *get along*?"

"What are you implying?"

"Leroy said he saw you and Violet at the Poco Dinero a couple months back."

"We danced some and shared a ride home."

"Must have been a long ride. You didn't come back till morning. I didn't think much of it till Leroy said something."

Cole thought he might have to find the talkative ranch hand and tell him to mind his own business, then decided bringing up that night would only make things worse.

"Want to go, Daddy," Nathan whined impatiently. He didn't like waiting.

"In a minute, son. I'm talking to Uncle Cole."

"Don't stay on my account," Cole said, seeing an opportunity to escape further scrutiny.

"Come on. Walk with me."

"I'm in the middle of feeding."

"The horses can wait ten minutes."

Cole would have manufactured another excuse, but he suddenly didn't want to. He and his brother had always been close, sharing everything, including careers and confidences. Cole could count on Josh to keep Vi's secret. Certainly for the next hour.

Besides, the fact was he could use some advice as well as a chance to unload. He'd grown tired of having only himself for counsel.

He and Josh set out on a course that circled the horse stables, Josh leading Hurry Up and his two young riders. The kids weren't interested in the grown-ups, allowing Cole and Josh to talk relatively freely.

Cole cut right to the chase. "Vi's pregnant."

"You're kidding!" Josh gaped at him. "Is it yours?"

"She told me Monday." Cole gave a brief account of what had happened then and yesterday at the doctor's office.

When he was done, Josh asked, "And you were together only the one night?"

"She didn't think we should date. Said it wasn't professional. That, and I think she considers me a flight risk, ready to leave at the drop of a hat."

"What are you going to do?"

"We haven't decided. She wants to wait."

"That must be why she called the meeting. To tell us she's pregnant."

"She's worried she might miscarry—it's happened before. Three times, back when she was married." Cole was growing fed up with circling the stables. His brother, however, appeared not to notice. Did people automatically start putting their children first when they became a parent?

Would Cole? "Her doctor gave her strict orders to rest every day and not work so hard. Do you suppose the ranch has a policy regarding medical leave?"

"No idea. Gabe will have to answer that. If not, we'll figure something out. She's a good employee. I can't imagine not trying to help her."

Cole agreed. Vi had told him she'd been just eighteen when she came to Dos Estrellas, the summer after high school. The Dempseys had taken her in, giving her a home as well as a job. Raquel loved her like family, as had Cole's late father.

Why hadn't he shown Cole and Josh that kind of love? Was the estrangement really all their mother's fault? She may have perpetuated it, but their dad hadn't fought it, either.

"Why do you think Dad hated us?" Cole hadn't intended to ask the question, it just slipped out.

"He didn't," Josh answered, in a somewhat tired voice. "The problem was him and Mom and their inability to get along."

Cole suspected there'd been much more going on, but let the subject drop. Josh had reconciled his differences with their father a while ago and didn't hang on like Cole. Perhaps because coming to Dos Estrellas had resulted in a safe, stable home for his children, a woman he loved and a job he'd come to believe was his calling.

Unfortunately, Cole was of a completely different mind. He liked cattle ranching well enough and someday might make it his living, but he still preferred busting broncs, training horses and chasing the sun to the next town.

"Are you remotely ready to be a dad?" Josh asked. "You haven't ever been the settling down kind."

"I want to be ready."

"You're going to have someone depending on you.

Someone who can't do the simplest of things for him or herself."

Cole glanced over his shoulder at his niece and nephew and tried to see himself as their parent. It wasn't easy. He'd been something of a drifter for the past twelve years.

"What if you made Mustang Valley your home base instead of Grandpa and Grandma's?"

Josh's suggestion was a reasonable one. Except for one problem.

"I'm not sure Vi wants me here. She made it clear she'd rather go it alone than have a part-time dad in the picture."

"She has a point. I tried that, and it didn't work. I wound up with an addict for a wife and two children who suffered from neglect. If you're not willing to fully commit, you might as well leave Violet to raise the baby by herself."

Cole heard what his brother said, and also what he didn't say: that if he failed to commit, he'd be just like their father, a man who'd abandoned his children.

Cole didn't think he could stand another similarity between them. There were already too many.

He kept watch for Vi's arrival, staying busy in the horse stables after finishing with the afternoon feeding. At last her pickup truck pulled into the driveway leading to the ranch.

He ignored the rush of relief coursing through him, along with the thrill of anticipation, and hurried to catch up. She was on her way to the house for their meeting. *Her* meeting.

"Hey, not so fast."

Glancing back, she stopped and waited. Cole took it as a good sign that she didn't race ahead.

"How are you doing?" He fell into step beside her.

"All right, I guess."

Her face told a different story. It had a pinched, exhausted look made worse by the dark circles beneath her eyes.

Cole repressed a sudden urge to wrap her in his arms. Or maybe not so sudden. He'd felt the same when she'd told him about her pregnancy. If anything, this protectiveness was becoming a habit.

"Did you get a chance to rest?" he asked.

"Not really."

"Too keyed up?"

"I'm not nervous."

He had his doubts. This couldn't be easy for her; it was a lot for anyone to handle.

"Did you at least put your feet up for a while?"

"I did." She smiled, though it was difficult to interpret. She might have been pleased Cole cared, or she might be placating him.

He noticed she held a spiral notebook in the crook of her arm. Had she organized her thoughts? He could picture her sitting in her living room recliner, feet up and furiously scribbling away.

"It's going to be fine," he assured her. "There's nothing Gabe won't do for you."

"What about you and Josh? Your votes count just as much as Gabe's."

"You know how I feel."

"Do I?"

"You're a great employee. You deserve time off."

"I see." She didn't mask the disappointment in her voice.

"What do you want me to say, Vi? That I care about you and what happens? I do. I hope you have this baby, and I hope it's born healthy. I'll do my best to be a good father and a good provider. Whatever you need from me. But you said yourself, you want to wait."

"You're right. That wasn't fair." She started to say more, then faltered, seemingly at a loss for words.

"This is new territory for both of us," he pointed out.

"Yeah, it is." This time, her smile was genuine. "Two months ago, I wouldn't have thought I'd be having this conversation with you."

"Me, either."

His response might have been a little too strong, for she grew abruptly quiet. Great. Well, too late now. They were at the ranch house.

They entered through the kitchen door, Cole waiting for Vi to go first. Raquel wouldn't be attending the meeting, but she'd put out an array of refreshments. On the counter were pitchers of iced tea and cold water, along with a basket of warm, fresh-baked sopapillas, and honey to drizzle on them.

Cole picked up a paper plate and lifted the cover keeping the sopapillas warm. Having no shame, he took two.

"Want one?" he asked Vi.

She grimaced. "No, thanks."

"Still nauseous?"

"It comes and goes." She hesitated a moment, then touched his arm in a brief but personal gesture. "See you in the meeting."

Cole watched her walk away, head held high and shoulders squared as if steeling herself for what lay ahead.

No sense waiting. Holding his plate of sopapillas, he cut across the kitchen to the dining room. That was where most meetings were conducted, along with Sunday and holiday dinners, which Raquel hosted with pleasure.

The house also had an office that once belonged to Cole's father. Before Gabe became engaged to Reese and started helping at the Small Change, he'd handled all the ranch finances and record keeping, sitting behind the desk their father once occupied.

In recent months, Josh had taken over the task. Cole rarely set foot in the office. He could barely balance his own personal checking account. The ranch finances, already shaky, would suffer further if he were to get involved.

Cole's brothers and Vi were already gathered in the brightly lit dining room by the time he wandered in. The three floor-to-ceiling windows let in the late-afternoon sun. If not for the air conditioner humming away, the room would have heated to an unbearable temperature.

Everyone glanced up at Cole's entrance, each of them wearing a different expression. Vi's was carefully contained, Josh's piqued with interest and Gabe's a mixture of mild confusion and curiosity. Then again, he was the only one who didn't know why Vi had called the meeting.

Cole took the seat beside Gabe and across from Vi. Josh sent him a private look that Cole interpreted as "Good luck."

Gabe caught the exchange, and his confusion visibly increased. Cole decided to let him stew. It would be better for all if he played dumb. The meeting was Vi's to run and the news hers to break. He was also still learning his way with his half brother. They'd become friends, which was a huge step from when Cole first arrived at Dos Estrellas. But they weren't close. Yet.

Gabe had loved their father, and why not? He was the son who'd grown up with August Dempsey. The son their father had taken under his wing and taught the cattle business, and who'd stayed by their father's side those long eighteen months while he'd been ill. The son who'd been promised the ranch.

For that reason, Gabe hadn't liked Cole and Josh when

they first met, seeing them as unwelcome intruders. But necessity had a way of making allies of would-be enemies. For their own different and very personal reasons, the three brothers had agreed to join forces and run the ranch together for a year. Hopefully, by then it would be operating in the black.

Cole had been waiting patiently for that day, when he'd be able to get his share of their inheritance and leave. With Vi's pregnancy, his plan might change.

Sweat seeped into his shirt collar, and he absently tugged at it. Was he on edge? Hell, yes. This wasn't just any family meeting. Vi was getting ready to rock their world.

In response to that thought, more sweat saturated his collar. He hadn't felt this way since the last time he'd ridden a bull.

Vi turned to a page in her notebook and glanced at the sheet. "If everyone's ready, we can get started."

Her statement was met with nods of agreement.

"Let's do it," said Gabe.

She swallowed. "I want to thank you for giving me some time off recently. As you know, my parents are getting a divorce, and it's not going amicably."

"If you need more time, take it." Gabe relaxed, no doubt thinking this was the reason for the meeting.

"I do, actually. And thank you."

"No problem."

"But not to visit them in Seattle. I, um, have some news. My own news. It's a bit unexpected. For everyone." She paused and swallowed again, careful to keep her features neutral. "I'm... I'm pregnant."

Gabe's jaw went slack, and he stared, dumbfounded. Josh tried to act surprised and did a passable job.

"You're right," Gabe said, and raked his fingers through

his dark hair. "This is unexpected. I guess congratulations are in order."

Vi attempted a smile. "I appreciate it."

"You're going to want time off when the baby's born?" Gabe was clearly struggling to understand. He shot a glance at both Cole and Josh. Neither of them made a comment.

"I saw my doctor yesterday," Vi said. "She recommended—insisted, really—that I work fewer hours and rest more." Finally, she glanced briefly at Cole and Josh. "As Gabe knows, I have a history of miscarriages. I'm hoping you'll agree to let me work half days for the foreseeable future. Naturally, you don't have to pay me for the time off."

Gabe didn't hesitate. Neither did he confer with Cole or Josh. "Of course. And we'll give you full pay."

"I can't ask that of you."

"You aren't asking. We're offering. And that includes after the baby's born."

Cole noticed Josh struggling to stay quiet. Dos Estrellas wasn't in a financial position to carry an employee who wasn't working full-time. Yet Vi had been with the ranch for over ten years. She deserved special consideration for her loyalty.

"No." Tears welled in her eyes, and she shook her head emphatically. "I won't accept pay if I'm not working. But I do have vacation and sick time coming."

"We'll figure something out," Gabe said.

"If I…if anything happens, then of course I'll come back to work full-time as soon as I'm able."

"Nothing will happen." Gabe didn't ask her to elaborate. "When are you having the baby?"

"Seven months. December."

Gabe furrowed his brows in concentration, as people

did when they were mentally counting backward. He, too, must have heard the gossip from Leroy, for he looked directly at Cole and didn't appear happy.

Cole waited for Vi to say something, naming him as the father, or for Gabe to straight out ask. Neither happened.

Vi continued after consulting her notebook. "The doctor says I can still work. Just no riding and no heavy lifting. I realize that describes about half my job. But I can still run errands, do the paperwork, make phone calls, meet with the vet. I can either work mornings or afternoons or split my shift with a break in the middle. Whatever's convenient for you."

"Let's see how it goes," Gabe said. "Take each week, each day as it comes."

"I want to make this as easy on everyone as possible." She read from her notebook, then cleared her throat. "I have a suggestion, if no one minds."

"Fire away."

"Since you're busy at the Small Change and Josh is tied up covering for you, I thought maybe Cole could take over some of my duties."

"Me?" He sat up straight. "I'm not qualified to be livestock manager."

"I'd still be in charge," Vi said. "Oversee your work like I do now."

"We'll all help you, Cole," Gabe said, as if it was a done deal.

"Sounds good to me," added Josh.

"Now, wait a minute—"

Gabe cut him off. "You're the best candidate. You have the most time and you're one of the ranch owners."

Cole didn't like being reminded he had a responsibility to the ranch. He damn well knew it.

"We could possibly find someone else," Vi said. "I know

one or two people looking for work. But you'd have to pay them, and can you really afford another expense?"

Gabe turned to face Cole. "We can't."

For a moment, Cole pictured himself flying out of the chute on the back of a bronc, ten feet off the ground, with one hand holding on to the bucking strap for dear life. His harsh breathing and pounding heart drowned out the cheers of the crowd. Then, all at once, the buzzer sounded.

Slowly, the picture faded as reality set in. There'd been so many changes to his life recently. Moving to Dos Estrellas. Cattle ranching. Vi and the baby.

Something told him this was only the beginning. If he was going to back out, now was the time.

"All right. I'll do it."

Chapter Four

Cole surveyed the manmade pond, noting that the water level had dropped two inches in the past two days. A total of fifteen inches in the past two weeks. Four months ago, a decrease in the level would have been expected, as Arizona had experienced its worst drought in decades.

But the drought had ended in February with a record-breaking deluge, followed by two more storm fronts passing through. Water levels shouldn't be a problem. The other livestock ponds on Dos Estrellas were at capacity, providing an ample supply of fresh water for the herds, both mustangs and cattle. The cause of this pond's depletion had yet to be determined, and Cole didn't have a clue.

He'd been relieving Vi of her more demanding duties for just under a week, having heard the concerns about the pond before today but not paying much attention. Now he was in charge, which was like expecting a first grader to solve a complex calculus equation.

He could call Vi and ask her opinion, except he didn't want to appear incompetent. Which he was, at least as far as livestock ponds went.

"Here. Check this out." Joey, one of the hands Cole frequently worked with, squatted next to the pond's edge and pointed to a spot in the dark, murky water.

Cole tied Hotshot to a low-hanging paloverde branch.

If he didn't, the horse would probably gallop off to join the mustangs grazing peacefully over the next ridge. This pond was in the heart of Cara's sanctuary, close to where Cole had first glimpsed Hotshot. He'd been impressed with the horse's potential, enough to seek out Cara the moment he returned to the ranch and ask to buy him.

She'd refused, striking a deal with him instead. In exchange for Hotshot, Cole helped her train other mustangs, preparing them for either adoption or use in her equine therapy program. Designed to benefit special-needs children, the program was officially launching at the end of the month.

Incredibly, it had already generated enough income from early enrollments to support the sanctuary through the end of the year, including paying the ranch a modest monthly rent. Little by little, they were chipping away at the mountain of bills, reducing it to a small hill.

If only Cole had more time. Training horses, especially roping and cutting horses, was his favorite pastime, next to rodeoing. But covering for Vi had become his first priority. She continued to be sick most days and was always tired.

"What is it?" he asked, going over to stand beside Joey.

"A leak."

"You're joking."

"'Fraid not."

"A pond can leak?" Cole had never heard of such a thing. He studied the spot Joey had indicated and noticed a small whirlpool, like water draining from a sink basin. Now and then a bubble or two rose to the surface.

"Somehow, the gravel bed's developed a crack," Joey said. "Water's seeping into the surrounding ground."

Joey was all of twenty-three years old but had been a ranch hand since he was fifteen and knew more than Cole could ever hope to learn. He was also one of two hands who hadn't quit when Cole's father died. Another reason to respect the young man.

"How does that happen?" Cole asked.

"One of the horse's feet could've punctured the bed."

He'd seen horses standing in the ponds, the water reaching their flanks. One rangy old fellow liked to swim. With enough force, it was possible a sharp hoof could puncture the bed.

"How do we fix it?"

"My grandpa used to pour borax into his ponds."

"Isn't that a detergent?"

Joey laughed, making Cole feel even more ignorant. "Technically, it's a mineral. Depending on how big the crack is, borax can plug it."

"You think the leak's caused by a crack?" Cole had learned only this morning that there was a complicated engineering system to these ponds. A faulty valve or rupture in the pipe could result in a costly repair, requiring the pond to be drained and reexcavated.

"Good place to start," Joey said. "And if the borax doesn't work, you haven't spent much money."

Cole was all for economizing. The ranch couldn't afford another expense, one possibly in the tens of thousands of dollars. While the pond was within the sanctuary boundaries, the land technically belonged to Dos Estrellas. Cost of repairs fell to the brothers.

"Guess I know where I'll be going this afternoon." He pushed to his feet. "Will you be ready to ride out again in the morning? Six sharp."

"Sure." Without confirming that they were done, Joey walked to where he'd left his horse tied.

Cole had the impression he'd been dismissed. Not the treatment a boss expected from his employee. Then again, it was hard to respect a boss who knew less than the employee about the job. The thought unsettled Cole. Funny, he wouldn't have cared about Joey's approval a week ago.

They mounted their horses and started out in the direction of the ranch, a good two-and-a-half-mile trek. Typically, they'd have taken the ranch ATVs when inspecting the pastures, but this particular pond was in a hard to reach location, and the vehicles sometimes got stuck in one of the deep ravines. Horses were simply better suited for this terrain.

Besides, Cole preferred traveling by horse. The scenery on this part of the ranch was spectacular. The distant McDowell Mountains, newly covered in a spring blanket of green cacti and brush, rose up to embrace a glorious, vivid blue sky. Pinnacle Peak, identifiable by its distinct angled shape, sat like a turret on a medieval castle.

If it weren't for the exceedingly warm temperatures, Cole would consider this paradise on Earth. No wonder his great-grandfather Dempsey had taken one look at Mustang Valley and decided it was the place to build the ranch of his dreams and raise his family.

Someday, Dos Estrellas would belong to Cole's child, Josh's two and Gabe's, if he had any. A fifth generation of Dempseys. But only if the ranch began turning a profit again. Otherwise, they'd be forced to sell at a loss, leaving little for the next generation.

Would it really matter? Money, having plenty or doing without, hadn't made a difference in Cole's life. All he'd wanted was a father.

What about his own child? If Cole left Mustang Valley, he'd be no better than his dad. Was that the legacy he really wanted to leave behind?

"If the borax doesn't work," Joey called to Cole, "Violet has the name of an engineer—"

"Don't talk to her yet. Let's give this a try. How long does borax usually take to plug a leak?"

"Days, if we're lucky. Could be a week or more. May take several tries, depending on the size of the leak. Good thing there's no rain in the forecast. That will make the pond level readings more accurate."

He and Joey continued along the winding trail single file, with Cole in the lead. Several of the mustangs grazing nearby lifted their heads to stare. A yearling colt pranced in circles around his mother, then stopped and reared, front hooves pawing the air. The sight might have been taken straight from history, a hundred years ago when wild mustang roamed this valley.

Cole's heart suddenly stirred. That, too, unsettled him. Why should he care so much about Dos Estrellas? It wasn't home.

But it was home to the people he *cared* about. His brother, niece and nephew and, yes, Vi.

As Cole and Hotshot passed a large patch of prickly pear cacti, a covey of quail resting there took flight, the whir of their flapping wings creating a loud noise. Startled, Hotshot lowered his head and started bucking. Cole immediately drew up on the reins, squeezed with his legs and put all his weight in his heels. Evidently, the horse wasn't as far along in his training as Cole had assumed.

Behind him, he heard Joey shout, "Whoa there," and hoped the kid's horse didn't also spook.

"Easy, boy." With practiced ease, Cole rode out the bucking spree. Bit by bit, Hotshot quieted. Soon enough, he was standing still, sides heaving and nostrils flaring.

Joey rode up behind him. "Well," he said, humor coloring his voice. "That was some fine riding. A body might think you rodeoed for a living."

Cole grinned and adjusted his cowboy hat, which he'd

nearly lost during the minor calamity. Then he and Hotshot walked on as if nothing out of the ordinary had happened.

"You miss the life?" Joey asked.

Cole didn't think before answering. "I do."

"I hear tell you're going back."

That had been the plan. "Might. It all depends."

"What are you going to do about a roping horse?"

Cole decided Joey wasn't being rude so much as he was curious, or simply killing time. It was no secret Cole had sold off his four champion roping horses and given the money to Gabe. Some of the younger steers had come down with a highly contagious virus last winter, and Gabe had used the money to purchase antibiotics.

Cole sometimes asked himself why he'd done it. Mostly for Josh. His older brother wanted to stay at Dos Estrellas and needed a home where he could bring his children to live.

But that wasn't the real reason or the most important one. As much as Cole wanted to be gone from Mustang Valley—*had* wanted to be gone—he refused to be called a quitter. When he left, it would be with the respect of his family and the ranch employees.

No one, especially Josh and Gabe, would give him that respect if he abandoned Vi and their child.

"I'm hoping Hotshot will prove himself," Cole said, his thoughts back to the present.

"He's a fine horse, but he has a long way to go."

"True enough." As the past few minutes had demonstrated.

Eventually, he and Joey reached the gate separating the mustang sanctuary from the cattle grazing lands. The herds were constantly moved from section to section in order to conserve grass and allow it to regenerate.

Last week, Cole had helped relocate the pregnant cows

in this section from one farther south. Most were due to deliver in late fall or early winter. This he'd learned from Vi, who, despite being a slip of a girl, was practically an expert on cattle. She credited Cole's father for teaching her.

Once through the gate, Cole and Joey resumed their trek across the section. In the distance, the roofs of the ranch house and outbuildings came into view. Two hills over, cattle grazed, appearing unaffected by the heat.

A cluster of paloverde trees grew to their left in a dry wash that had been full and running three months ago. Birds perched in the treetops, hopping nervously from branch to branch. Cole kept one eye glued to the ground, on the lookout for rattlesnakes and lizards hidden among the rocks.

All at once a low, mournful bellow carried over to them from behind the trees.

Cole drew up on the reins. "What's that?"

"A cow." Joey was already turning his horse in the direction of the sound.

Cole followed. "You sure?"

"Trust me, it is."

Reaching the trees, they dismounted and pushed branches aside to investigate. Joey had been right. The cow stood with her head down, guarding the lifeless body of her prematurely born calf.

"Oh, man," Cole said, his shoulders slumping. The poor thing never had a chance.

"You stay here with the cow," Cole told Joey, after they'd taken time to assess the situation. "I'll ride to the ranch, get my truck and see who's available to help. We'll load the calf in the back, and you lead the cow to the ranch. I think the vet should check her out, just to be on the safe side."

He headed to where Hotshot was tied, trying to remember if the vet's number was programed into his phone.

"Sounds good," Joey said.

Both of them had kept a reasonable distance from the cow in case she became aggressive. Her calf may not have survived, but there were no guarantees she'd willingly abandon it.

Finding a patch of shade to escape the sweltering heat, Joey pulled out his cell phone. "I'll call Violet."

Cole ground to a halt. "Don't do that."

"Shouldn't she know? She's in charge."

All Cole could think about was how news of the premature calf might upset her. She already struggled with mood swings—her words, not his. News like this would have her leaping out of bed or off the recliner, wherever she happened to be resting, and racing to the rescue.

"I'll call her," Cole said, though he wouldn't until later. Much later.

It was too hot to gallop Hotshot, but that didn't stop Cole from trotting him the last mile to the ranch. There, he located Leroy, the wrangler who had blabbed about Cole and Vi leaving the bar together, and, handing over the reins, instructed him to look after Hotshot.

"Make sure he's cooled down before you put him up."

"Will do."

"You seen Josh?"

"Said he was going to the house."

Cole found his brother in the office, staring at the computer screen. He glanced up the second Cole entered. "I swear I'm going cross-eyed staring at these spreadsheets."

"Forget them. We have a problem."

Josh stood. Cole was still feeding him details as they climbed into his truck. After a quick stop at the tack room for a plastic tarp, they sped out the gate leading to the pastures and up the dirt road toward the hills, clouds of dust spewing from the rear tires. Minutes later, the road narrowed to a horse trail and the going got rough.

"What are you doing?" Josh asked when Cole drove the truck off the trail and onto rocky, uneven land thick with low-growing vegetation.

"Taking a shortcut."

"Are you sure about this?" Josh anchored one hand on the dash to keep himself from coming off the seat when they bounced over a rotted tree trunk.

"Hang on," Cole warned. "There's a gully ahead."

Joey was still waiting in the same patch of shade when they arrived, thankfully in one piece. Cole credited his driving skills. Josh had a different opinion.

Together, the three of them devised a plan. Cole would rope the cow. Hopefully, she'd come willingly—she already appeared to be losing interest in the calf. Just to be sure, they'd brought along a bucket of grain as added incentive. As soon as Joey left with the cow, Cole and Josh would take care of the calf.

Cole reached behind the seat for his lariat. He seldom went anywhere without it, a habit he'd formed years ago. Automatically adjusting the size of the loop, he slowly approached the cow, who stared at him with trepidation. About twenty feet away, he stopped. Josh and Joey watched from the truck.

"Come on, old girl." Cole raised the lariat over his head. "There's a bucket of grain waiting for you when this is all over."

It took only one try for Cole to lasso the cow. She resisted at first, shaking her head and bellowing angrily. Then she resigned herself to her fate and followed the tug on the rope to the feed bucket Josh held out.

Once Joey and the cow were on their way, Cole and Josh

gathered up the premature calf, wrapped it in the tarp and placed it in the truck bed. The vet might want to inspect the remains in order to determine what, if anything, had caused the cow to abort.

Because he was in a hurry, Cole took the same bumpy shortcut home. Josh pressed a hand to the crown of his hat, holding it in place.

"You must like living dangerously."

"I'd rather get this handled before Vi returns for her afternoon shift," Cole said. This week, she'd been working two hours in the morning and two hours in the afternoon, with a trip home in between.

"How's she doing?"

"Still sick, but the baby seems fine. She's being very careful."

"That's good. She must be relieved."

"I don't think she'll stop worrying until the baby's born."

"Have you two decided on anything yet?"

"We haven't had much time to talk. I did call that attorney, though." Their future sister-in-law, Reese, had recommended him. "The guy sounds knowledgeable enough, and what he said made sense."

"I hear a but."

"He's abrupt. This is a baby we're talking about, not a piece of property Vi and I are sharing."

Josh chuckled. "And so it begins."

"What?"

"Step one to being a father."

Cole didn't know how to respond. Was he really starting to see himself in the role of a father? Sometimes he felt as if he was simply doing what was expected of him. The baby had yet to become real. Eventually that would change, right?

"I still think she could do a lot better than me," he said.

"Don't underestimate yourself, buddy. My kids love you."

"Just goes to show, humans under the age of three aren't very good judges of character."

Josh laughed again, only to curse when he banged his elbow on the passenger door. "Hey, watch it—slow down!"

"Sorry. I just want to get there."

"Maybe you should take the main trail."

Cole steered down an incline toward a shallow ravine, brush and branches scraping the windows. The truck rocked as they climbed over and drove around obstacles. As they reached the bottom of the gulch, the right front tire got caught in a rut, causing them to lurch violently. A loud bang sounded.

Cole swore and hit the brakes, sending them into a skid.

"What did we run over?" Josh was already rolling down his window and sticking his head out.

"Not sure."

Frustrated with himself, Cole shoved open his door and stepped out. The truck was sitting at an angle that boded no good, and his frustration escalated when he saw the dent in the front bumper and the flattened front tire.

Josh came around to join him, took one look and let out a low whistle. "Got a spare? Going to be hard, changing a tire with the truck bottomed out."

"We're not changing the tire." He had seen this type of accident before, when a friend ran his vehicle into a ditch. Cole would bet money there was damage to the suspension system, and changing the tire could potentially cause more. He swore again, louder this time.

"A tow?"

"Yes, dammit." He could already imagine the cost. Getting a tow truck all the way out here wouldn't be cheap.

"Maybe Gabe can help."

Cole called him, and lucky for them, he did help. Reese worked at the local bank as assistant manager and had a customer with an auto-repair shop. They were only too glad to send their tow truck and offer a "friend discount." Cole thanked Reese profusely when she phoned him with the news.

"Sorry, but you'll have to wait a couple hours," she said. "They're on a call right now."

"No problem."

"I can send Joey back with food and water."

"You hungry?" Cole asked Josh, already knowing the answer. It was pushing one o'clock, and they'd missed lunch. Cole was still too mad at himself to eat.

"Starving," Josh said, wiping sweat from his brow. By now, they were both covered in grime.

"Thanks, Reese." Cole disconnected after saying good-bye.

Twenty minutes later, an ATV appeared in the distance. As it drew nearer, Cole recognized the driver and groaned. Vi, not Joey, was at the wheel. Reese must have called her.

Cole kicked at a rock. This day was going from bad to worse.

"You're a sight for sore eyes," Josh said when she pulled up and cut the engine. "What did you bring?" He was already heading for the ice chest strapped to the rack behind the seat.

"Sandwiches and soda."

"You're a lifesaver."

"Looks like you had quite a mishap." Vi climbed off the ATV and went over to examine Cole's truck.

Rather than reply, Cole dug inside the ice chest for a soda, popped the lid and guzzled the contents. The cool liquid soothed his parched throat but not his annoyance.

He'd driven recklessly solely to avoid Vi's seeing the calf, and it had made no difference. She was here, anyway.

"Keep her away from the truck bed," he told Josh under his breath, hoping Joey hadn't screwed up and told her. "She'll just get upset."

"Gotcha."

Vi came toward them, wearing a wry smile. "Can I ask why you decided to drive through the ravine?"

"A shortcut," Cole said.

"I don't think it worked."

"You're enjoying this, aren't you?"

She shrugged. "A little."

"How are you feeling? Are you sure it's okay to drive an ATV?"

Josh had meandered off to lean against the other side of the truck while he ate. Either he was trying to avoid the sun or was giving Cole and Vi some privacy.

"Not bad today. And, yes, it's okay, as long as I don't go off-road. I checked with Dr. Medina." Vi reached for the ice chest, struggling to lift the lid.

"Here, let me get that." Cole lifted it with ease, and she grabbed a bottled water.

"Thanks." Twisting off the lid, she asked, "Aren't you hungry?"

"I'll eat later."

Her gaze returned to the truck. "I hope you have good insurance."

"I can't believe I was that stupid."

She sat on the ATV's seat. "You must have been in a hurry."

"Isn't that how most accidents occur? Someone's in a rush."

"What's wrapped in the tarp?"

Cole was quick to respond. "Nothing."

"Really?" She craned her neck. "Because it looks like something. And with the way you were apparently hauling ass back to the ranch, I'd say it was something significant."

"Vi, it's nothing," he repeated, afraid that if he made a big deal, she'd become even more curious.

"Fine." She pushed herself off the seat. "I'll just take a look for myself."

"No." He grabbed her hand. "Trust me, you don't want to see. It's…" He decided a response close to the truth might dissuade her. "It's an animal carcass."

"Oh."

"We didn't want the coyotes to come after it."

Just when he thought she'd bought his story, suspicion flared in her eyes. "Does this have anything to do with Joey bringing back one of the cows? I saw him on the way here but I didn't stop to ask."

Cole attempted to distract her with teasing. "You were eager to see me?"

To his surprise, she answered seriously. "I was concerned."

"Really? I'm glad."

"That I was concerned?"

"Yes." He tugged on a stray lock of her silky hair.

"Don't make more of it than it is." She brushed his hand away. "Have a sandwich, Cole."

He did. But when he turned around, still holding the sandwich, he saw Vi at the side of the truck, lifting the tarp.

"No! Wait."

He rushed over, reaching her as she dropped the tarp and averted her head. An instant later, she stumbled away from him, bent over and heaved.

Chapter Five

"Why didn't you tell me?" Violet stared angrily at Cole.

"I was afraid you'd be upset. Which you were. Are," he amended.

She didn't relent. "I need to know when things like this happen. It's my job."

"I planned on telling you."

"When? After you and Josh disposed of the calf's remains?"

"Is that so bad?"

She supposed not, but she remained silent. Turning her truck onto the ranch grounds, she drove straight to her usual parking spot in the shade behind the horse stables.

They'd played a game of musical vehicles earlier. The tow truck arrived sooner than expected, just as Cole finished telling her about finding the cow and its baby. Joey had driven her pickup ahead of the tow truck in order to lead the way.

Once Cole's damaged pickup had been loaded onto the tow truck—Violet still couldn't believe he'd driven into the ravine like that; the guy didn't have a lick of sense—and the calf remains transferred to Violet's truck, they'd all driven home in a single, long caravan, with Josh on the ATV, Joey in the tow truck with the driver and Violet and Cole bringing up the rear.

No one had asked if the two of them were riding together. It had been assumed. She wasn't sure what to make of that or how she felt. Had news of her pregnancy leaked? She'd specifically asked the brothers not to say anything until she gave the okay.

"I already called the vet," Cole said.

"Good."

"Do you think this is the only incident?" Cole knew, as she did, that some bovine viruses caused spontaneous abortions in cows.

He was trying to distract her, keep her talking so she wouldn't dwell on the image of the calf. Little did he know he had only to smile and she'd forget her own name.

"We'll know for sure by the end of the week. Once we inspect the entire herd and search for stillborn calves."

There were literally hundreds of pregnant cows spread across hundreds of acres. The job would be a big one and require days.

"I'll handle it," Cole said.

"With my help."

"Under your direction, Vi. Leave the actual work to me."

She swung into her parking space, letting the motor idle and the air-conditioning run full blast. "You don't have the time. Not with doing half my job on top of yours."

"Josh and Gabe will pitch in."

"Do you even know what signs to look for?"

"I will." He grinned. "After you tell me. We can start tomorrow when Joey and I get back from the pond."

"Fine. Let me check the cow, then we'll decide on our next step. There's a map of the ranch in the supply shed with the different sections outlined. Might come in handy."

The shed also housed a battered old desk in the corner that she and the hands used when they needed a place to work, along with a cot, where more than one tired body had crashed when no other place was available.

"Tell me about the pond and what's causing the level to drop."

They walked to the corral where Joey had left the cow. The same corral where Vi had come upon Cole roping the steer the day he'd figured out she was pregnant.

Hard to believe nearly two weeks had passed since then. She was almost ten weeks pregnant. Ten weeks! Far enough along to start hoping, but not far enough to stop worrying. Every little cramp, every twinge, had her rushing to the bathroom to see if she'd started spotting. Thankfully, so far, she hadn't.

She'd been tempted to blurt the news last night when her mother called. Then, as usual, the complaining had begun. It seemed Violet's father wanted to sell their house and split the proceeds rather than give it to her mother in the divorce settlement.

Violet had only half listened. She'd heard enough bickering from her parents over the years to fill every room in the house. They were equally to blame for their unhappiness and their bitter divorce.

She'd let her mother dominate the conversation for another ten minutes before making up an excuse and ending the call. Next time, she'd tell her about the baby. If nothing bad happened between now and then.

"Joey seems to think a leak is responsible," Cole said.

Violet nodded, focusing on the present rather than the past. "That makes sense."

"You've heard of ponds leaking before?"

"They're manmade, which means they can, for lack of a better word, break."

He grunted, then went on to explain Joey's suggestion of using borax. Violet hadn't heard of that before, but thought the idea had merit.

"I was planning on running to the hardware store in town this afternoon to buy some," Cole said. "I'll go tonight instead."

"I can pick up a box on my way home."

"No, I'll do it. I have to stop by the repair shop and go over the estimate on my truck with them before they'll start."

He looked tired. Was she working him too hard? "You okay?" she asked.

"I'm sorry about the calf. I wanted to spare you. It was a pretty grisly sight."

He was right, but that hadn't excused her emotional display in front of Cole and Josh—her stomach revolting, followed by a few moments of tears. This was hardly the first time she'd seen a deceased calf. They might think her too tenderhearted, or incapable of handling her job.

At the corral, she and Cole stopped in front of the fence. The cow stood beneath the metal shade, staring into space and wearing—Violet was convinced—a forlorn expression on her pretty brown-and-white face. Some might accuse Violet of projecting her own feelings onto the cow. They wouldn't be far off.

"She doesn't appear to be sick," Violet said.

"No," Cole agreed. "Maybe there's no explanation."

She'd heard that often enough from her own doctor when her babies hadn't thrived. It didn't help, then or now.

"Thank you." She turned to Cole. "For thinking of me."

"I think of you a lot. And the baby."

Her curiosity got the best of her. "Do you?"

"In fact, I think about that night a lot."

As if it wasn't hot enough outside already, her cheeks instantly heated beneath his intense scrutiny.

"Hmm. The sex."

"Not the sex." He dipped his head. "Though it was good. Mighty good."

"Cole, we can't." She moved away, putting some much needed distance between them.

He stopped her with a gentle tug on her elbow. "What I think about is the talking. The holding. The sleeping in each other's arms and waking up with you beside me. The smell of your hair and the softness of your skin."

She could feel her resistance slowly melting. He'd had that effect on her practically from the moment they'd met. It had required all her willpower to keep her intense attraction to him a secret those first few months.

Then he'd appeared in the crowd one night at the Poco Dinero Bar. A night when her defenses had been particularly low after a call from her parents. He'd squeezed in next to her at the booth, then asked her to dance. He'd made her laugh. Forget her troubles. Kissed her senseless in the parking lot. The attraction she'd fiercely kept at bay had burst free.

Today, like then, it hovered precariously close to the surface, barely contained. Cole was the temptation she craved and couldn't resist, made all the more difficult by his fingertips caressing her arm.

"This can't happen," she insisted. "It won't lead to anything good."

"What's happening, Vi?" He inched closer. "Tell me."

"You know."

"I do. I just want to hear you say it."

Her body yielded in response to his coaxing, and the desire to flee vanished. She could, quite easily, let herself sink into his embrace. She would, too, if he kissed her. History had proved how susceptible she was to him. His touch. His caring.

"We're forgetting what's important," she said. "The baby. Our future. The decisions we need to make."

"I'm not forgetting. Far from it." His hand slid up her arm. Tingles erupted in the wake of his fingertips.

She lifted her chin and stared, captivated by his striking blue eyes. A man didn't deserve eyes that gorgeous.

A smile tugged at his mouth. A mouth she knew firsthand was skilled at many wonderful things, kissing being only one of them.

She closed her eyes, drawing on the last of her slim reserve. "What if someone sees us?"

"You're making excuses. No one's around."

Where were Josh and Joey when she needed them?

"I might be making excuses," she said, "but they're valid ones."

"Don't you ever just go with the flow? Seize the moment?"

"Seizing the moment is what got me pregnant."

He chuckled. Before she quite knew it, he'd wrapped a strong arm around her waist and lifted her flush against him. She was forced to hold on to his shoulders or risk losing her balance.

He waited till she met his gaze. "Last chance."

No, no, no.

Her silent protest was useless. The next instant, his lips covered hers and parted them. His tongue met no resistance and slid into her mouth, tangling with hers.

Yes, yes, yes, she thought and willingly took the lead.

This was much better than in the parking lot. Better than when they'd arrived at her house and he'd walked her to the door. Better than when she'd invited him inside, then into her bedroom, where he'd made incredible, delicious love to her. Better than her imagination, and she'd been imagining all sorts of scenarios recently, each of them involving her and Cole and endless expanses of naked skin.

She was a terrible person. To let him do this to her. To be doing this to him. To be wanting more.

Her arms went around his neck and she hung on, needing him to keep her anchored lest she float away. Sounds filled her ears. Her breathing. His heart pounding. Her name on his lips right before he took the kiss to the next level. Then, neither of them were making a sound as she gave herself over to him completely.

When she would have gone on indefinitely, let him take any and every advantage, he suddenly stopped.

"What's wrong?"

Had she really just asked that? Of course they should stop. They were crazy to have started in the first place. At least he'd come to his senses. She'd been ready to jump once again off the deep end.

This time, she did pull away, and he let her go.

"Vi. Please." He paused. "I was thinking of you. A kiss is one thing, but this isn't the right time or place to..."

He was right, of course. She, as much as him, had gotten carried away.

Acutely embarrassed, she averted her head. "I'm sorry. That shouldn't have happened."

"Hey, come on, now. Let's not have any of that."

"Any of what?"

He bent his head close to her. "Feeling bad. Regrets. We kissed because there's something undeniable between us."

"Yeah, a baby."

"Feelings, Vi. Strong ones."

He was right, and that was what scared her. She could have this baby with him, walk the delicate line between personal and business, as long as they kept their relationship casual.

Violet wanted to believe in the institution of marriage and that happy families weren't a myth or the basis of a TV sitcom. But she'd grown up in a dysfunctional household and become the unwilling collateral damage of two parents determined to foist their misery on everyone else. She honestly didn't know if she was capable of sustaining a healthy relationship with a man. Hadn't her and Denny's marriage gone down in flames?

Even scarier, what if she let Cole into her heart, made a commitment to him, only to lose the baby? What then? Would guilt cause him to stay with her despite his desire to return to the rodeo circuit? And if he did stay, he might very well grow to resent her.

Arm's length. That was where she needed to keep him. For both their sakes.

"Come on," she said. "Let's look at the map."

"I'LL TAKE A couple of those."

Cole returned the serving spoon to the bowl of refried beans and stared pointedly at Gabe. "Your hand broken?"

Gabe dropped into a chair at the kitchen table. "Figured if you were already making yourself lunch, you could fix me some, too. Not like it's work."

Bean burritos. Raquel, not Cole, had prepared the fixings earlier in the day before taking Josh's two kids with her to visit her friend in Mesa. They'd be gone until late afternoon. While the family usually ate breakfast and dinner together, lunch was a fend-for-yourself affair, depending on what each of them had scheduled for the day.

"One or two?" Cole asked.

He was in too good a mood to let anything or anyone spoil it, and had been that way since yesterday. His kiss with Vi was the reason. She may have tried afterward to pretend nothing happened, but something *had* happened.

Something he was convinced she'd enjoyed as much as he had.

"Two." Gabe poured himself a glass of ice water.

Cole took two more tortillas from the warmer, slapped them on a plate and passed it to Gabe. He could add his own beans and condiments.

Josh entered the kitchen from outside. "Hey, that looks good. Count me in."

"Since when did I become the cook?" Cole grumbled.

"It's refried beans on a tortilla." Josh pulled out the chair between his two brothers and sat. "How hard can it be?"

Cole was sure Raquel had spent hours preparing the homemade tortillas and beans and assembling the fixings— shredded cheese, salsa, jalapeños and diced onions.

He went to the pantry and found an open bag of corn chips, which he set in the middle of the table. His brothers attacked the food like starving animals, whereas he tried to show at least a modicum of decorum.

It wasn't often the three of them were alone in the house. At one time that would have created an awkward and unbearable situation. These days, they might not always agree, but they handled their disputes like adults rather than bickering children.

"How's Violet?" Gabe asked between bites.

Cole stopped, the burrito inches from his mouth. Did Gabe suspect anything? Had he seen Cole and Vi kissing?

"Fine. She worked all morning, then went home a while ago for the rest of the day."

"I saw her helping Leroy unloading supplies."

"You did?" Cole frowned. "She's supposed to be taking it easy. No lifting"

"She was. Taking it easy. Sort of."

"What does that mean?"

"Nothing heavy. Some sacks and cartons."

Cole decided to call Vi after lunch just to check on her. On second thought, he'd drop by instead.

"You two getting along okay?" Josh asked.

Again Cole's suspicions were roused, and he answered hesitantly. "Great."

"She's easy to work with." Josh snatched the bag of corn chips and dumped a second large helping onto his paper plate, along with a heaping serving of salsa.

Cole almost laughed. "Are you kidding? She's a taskmaster and a perfectionist. Riding a bull is less work and less daunting."

"She might make a rancher out of you yet," Gabe mumbled between mouthfuls.

Remarks like that, ones implying Cole would eventually settle down and stay at Dos Estrellas, usually filled him with the urge to hit the road and the next town, pausing only long enough to pack his bags. Instead, he sat where he was, wondering if the feeling washing over him was contentment. It had been so long...

"I heard you and Joey fixed the leak in the pond." Gabe bit into his second burrito.

"Joey's the one who came up with the idea."

"Whoever did, it's working."

"Let's not get ahead of ourselves," Cole cautioned. It was true, the pond level had been holding since yesterday, but it was much too soon to consider the plug secure and the problem resolved.

"That was pretty clever, though. Borax, huh?"

Cole shook his head. "I wouldn't have thought of it."

They stayed sitting at the table even after their lunch was consumed. Cole studied his brothers while trying not to be obvious.

What would their father think, seeing the three of them getting along and acting like, well, brothers? He'd probably smile and say that was his plan all along and the reason he'd left a third of Dos Estrellas to each of his sons rather than entirely to Gabe, as he'd always promised.

Would the ranch continue to do well without Cole if he left and returned to the rodeo circuit? Had he made any significant contributions, besides selling his roping horses last fall to generate revene, or had he simply been another pair of hands to help with the work and lighten the load?

If he returned to the circuit? Wait a minute. At what point during these past few months had his thinking changed?

Getting along with his brothers was part of the reason, he supposed. But there was also the baby to consider. Both the good example set by Josh and the bad example set by their father had Cole feeling his place might just be with Vi and their child rather than on the road.

There was also their recent kiss. It had affected him even more than making love with her. Their night together had been spontaneous, the result of circumstances neither of them anticipated. The kiss, however, was deliberate, the result of an affection far more profound than simple attraction.

That was not to say the sex hadn't been satisfying. How could it be anything else? Vi was soft and curvy and, once she let down her guard, full of passion. But, just as he'd told her earlier, what he remembered best about their night together, what had mattered the most, was the intimate emotional connection they'd shared.

Funny, since Cole had a commitment phobia and tended to avoid those aspects of a relationship whenever possible. Plenty of women had accused him of running scared. Vi might be among them if he wound up leaving Mustang Valley. But what choice did he have if he wanted to earn enough money to support their child?

"When will you be done?" Josh asked.

"Sorry." Cole hadn't been listening. "Done with what?"

"Inspecting the pregnant cows."

"Oh, right. End of the day tomorrow, I hope."

So far, none of the other pregnant cows appeared to have lost their calves. It was the kind of news they'd needed to hear.

"If you need help," Josh said, "give me a holler."

"I might take you up on that—" Cole was interrupted by his cell phone ringing. "Hang on a second." Seeing Vi's number on the display, he felt his heart rate spike. "Hi. How goes it?"

"Cole." Panic filled her voice. "Something's wrong."

"What?" He was already shoving his chair back from the table. Had another cow aborted? Had the cattle broken through a hole in the fence and gotten onto the neighbor's property?

"I'm bleeding."

Cripes. He should have thought of her first. What a moron.

"The baby…" She broke into sobs.

"Did you call 9-1-1?"

"We're too far out. You can drive me to the hospital faster. Dr. Medina said she'll meet us there."

Cole started for the door, fishing his keys from his jeans pocket, only to remember his truck was in the repair shop. "Hang tight. I'm on my way." He moved the phone away from his mouth. "Josh, I need to borrow your truck."

"What's wrong?"

"It's Vi. She's bleeding."

"Here." Josh tossed him his keys.

"I'll call you after I know more." Cole pushed through the kitchen door and broke into a run.

Vi's house was a short ten-minute drive away. Short any other day. Right now, he couldn't get there fast enough and was grateful for only one stop sign in town to slow him down. Sweat pouring from his brow, he screeched to a stop on the street in front of her driveway. Without bothering to knock, he entered the house on the same wave of adrenaline that had carried him from Dos Estrellas.

"Vi! Where are you?"

"In here."

He followed the sound of her voice to the living room. For the briefest fraction of a second, he recalled the two of them sitting on her overstuffed couch, unable to keep their hands off each other. Moments later, Vi had invited him into her bedroom.

The memory vanished at the sight of her lying on the couch, her legs elevated on a stack of decorative throw pillows.

"Are you all right?" He went to her side and crouched down.

"I still have cramps but the bleeding's lessened. For now," she added, her voice troubled, her green eyes glistening with unshed tears.

"Let's go." Without waiting for her to answer, he stood and picked her up as if she were a small child, one arm supporting her back, the other behind her knees.

"I can walk, Cole."

He didn't listen and headed for the door.

"My purse!" she cried out.

"Where is it?"

"The kitchen counter."

She insisted on locking the house behind them, though he was too anxious to care. Settling her in the passenger seat, he buckled the seat belt, then raced around to the driver's side.

"Thank you," she said, when they were on the road.

"No problem."

The look she gave him tore his heart in two. "I'm scared, Cole."

He reached across the console to cup her cheek, wishing he could do more to reassure her. "It's going to be okay, sweetie."

She covered his hand with hers, visibly trying to compose herself. "Let's hurry."

He needed directions to the hospital in Scottsdale. They'd barely reached the outskirts of Mustang Valley when he insisted she recline her seat as much as possible and elevate her feet. She said little on the drive, other than "turn left" or "take this street, it's quicker." He glanced over at her often, alarmed by the sight of her pale face.

"How you doing?" he asked, when they were about a mile away.

"Hanging in there." She looked more on the verge of a breakdown.

Not for the first time, he admired her courage and determination, something he'd seen her display often on the job. This, however, was different. Courage and determination in the face of a personal crises required incredible fortitude and strength of character. She had plenty of both.

She gazed worriedly out the window. "I shouldn't have helped Leroy with those supplies."

"You didn't lift anything heavy, right?"

"No. Still, it was stupid. What if I…" She sobbed softly. "I'll never forgive myself."

"Nothing's gone wrong yet."

Luck was on their side when they arrived at the hospital. Cole would gladly have blocked the emergency entrance in order to save time, but because of a nearby available space, Josh's truck would be spared a towing today.

Vi insisted on walking the short distance across the

parking lot to the front entrance, when he would have carried her. Their sedate pace nearly drove him crazy.

Inside, they went straight to the check-in desk. As soon
as Vi told the nurse on duty about her condition and symptoms, a wheelchair was produced and a stocky male attendant ordered her to sit.

"Ready for a ride?" he asked.

Cole stood there, unsure what to do next.

"Isn't your husband coming with us?"

"He's not my—"

"Yes, I'm coming," Cole said, and went with Vi, holding her hand as they traveled the corridor. To his great relief, she didn't correct the attendant.

Chapter Six

Cole didn't leave Vi's side. Not during the initial exam, which included the taking of her medical history. Not during the ultrasound, where seeing on the screen the blurry, gray image that was his child nearly caused his chest to explode. And not when Vi's doctor finally delivered the encouraging news that all appeared normal and the bleeding had stopped.

Vi burst into tears, and Cole held on to the bed rail for support. He hadn't realized how worried he was until this moment.

"I can't stress enough that you get sufficient rest," Dr. Medina said. "Stay in bed the next three days. Do not get out for any reason other than to shower or use the restroom. No more than one hour a day on your feet."

"I'll chain her down if necessary," Cole promised.

"I'd like to see you on Friday, just for a quick follow-up."

"We'll be there." Cole didn't seek Vi's permission before including himself.

"Call me, day or night, if there's any more spotting or cramping."

Vi nodded. Cole made a mental note to get the doctor's number from her.

"Should I stay with her tonight?" he asked.

Dr. Medina visibly missed a beat before answering. She had probably assumed Cole and Vi lived together.

Recovering quickly, she said, "Yes, that would be wise. Perhaps for the next few days."

Cole half expected Vi to complain, but she didn't.

Dr. Medina reviewed a long list of instructions with them before saying she'd complete the paperwork for Vi's discharge. Until the nurse came for her, she was to stay right where she was.

"Thank you," Cole said to the doctor as she left.

"You take good care of her."

"Yes, ma'am."

His plan was to stick to Vi's side for as long as necessary.

Maybe he *should* move in with her until the baby was born. Or at least until she passed the three-month mark. He studied her and tried to anticipate her reaction if he suggested it.

She appeared to be dozing as her eyes were closed and her face turned toward the wall. An empty chair sat beside the bed and he lowered himself into it. Earlier, he'd removed his cowboy hat. Now he plunked it on his head and gave the brim a firm tug.

The hat felt familiar and comfortable, like an old friend. He and this hat had been through a lot together. Rodeo wins and losses. Good times, bad times. Heartbreaks. Triumphs. Disappointments. He'd been wearing this hat when he got the news of his father's death. Also when he learned he'd inherited a third of Dos Estrellas and again when he found out Vi was pregnant.

With luck, the hat would be with him when he became a father for the first time.

Cole closed his eyes and conjured up the fuzzy image on the ultrasound screen. Was that really a child? His and

Vi's? If he concentrated hard, he could discern a human shape. Head. Body. Even tiny arms and legs.

In that moment, Cole was struck with a wonder he'd never experienced before. Together, he and Vi had made a baby. Small now, but one day, a child he could bounce on his knee. Teach to ride and rope. Pass on his share of the ranch, if he didn't sell to his brothers.

Was rodeoing what he truly wanted? He'd been so sure a short time ago. Now, he didn't know. In large part because he questioned Vi's feelings for him. She'd said she wanted him to remain in Mustang Valley. That might, however, only be as a responsible father who shared child-rearing duties. Not a romantic partner. Not a husband. Not a lover.

"Go home if you want," she said softly. "I can manage alone."

His head snapped up. "Like hell I'm leaving."

"Raquel will be happy to help. Or Cara."

"You and the baby are my responsibility."

She studied him, her eyes unreadable and her tone carefully neutral. "Do you mean that?"

"Yes. And not just financially. I'm going to take care of you. Both of you." Although at the moment, he didn't know how he'd accomplish that.

She glanced away.

"What did I say wrong?" It seemed he was always putting his foot in his mouth.

"Nothing."

"Then what's the matter?"

"I'm just being emotional."

He didn't doubt that, but he was also certain he'd disappointed her. He would have preferred to talk further, but just then the nurse whipped the curtain aside. "Are you ready to go home?" the young woman in scrubs asked brightly.

Vi left the hospital with a thick stack of papers Cole had every intention of reading when they reached her house. She was seated in a wheelchair and taken by the nurse from her room to the front entrance, where Cole waited, his truck idling. This time, she didn't refuse his help, and he assisted her into the passenger seat.

"There's a futon bed in my spare room," she said as they left the parking lot and merged with traffic.

"I can bunk on the couch."

"Wherever you're more comfortable."

He thought he might be more comfortable in *her* bed, but didn't comment. "I'll pick up something for dinner."

"I have food in the house."

"That's great. Except I can't cook."

"No problem. I have a ton of frozen dinners in the freezer." At his wry look, she added, "I'm busy and too tired when I get home to fix a big meal."

"Can you? Fix a meal?" They'd talked about many things, but cooking had never come up. Not once.

"If you're curious about whether I'm any good at it, I'm not."

"Then I guess we'll be eating out a lot, because I can barely boil an egg."

She smiled. Really smiled, and her twin dimples appeared. Cole swore he sank a little further under her spell. He hoped, should they have a girl, that she'd take after Vi and inherit those same stunning dimples.

"Have you thought about what you want?" he asked.

"For dinner?" Vi glanced his way.

He laughed. "A boy or a girl."

"Oh, I don't care. Not to be unoriginal, but I just want a healthy baby." She hesitated, her demeanor suddenly shy. "What about you? Do you have a preference?"

"None."

"Really?"

"Vi." He stopped at the streetlight, reached for her hand and raised it to his lips. "Really."

Sensing the tension coursing through her—or was it anticipation?—he let go, regretful when she returned her hand to her lap. Maybe he'd rushed her. He vowed to go slower the next time.

Several miles passed with Cole concentrating on the road while Vi reclined and appeared to be resting. At the outskirts of Mustang Valley, he offered a suggestion.

"I'll drop you off, get you situated in bed, then head to the ranch for some clothes and a toothbrush."

"What about the cows? You haven't finished checking them."

"It can wait until tomorrow. Besides, there's not enough daylight left." Their trip to the emergency room had taken the better part of the afternoon.

"You are going to work tomorrow," she stated. "We can't both be off."

"I'll go. After I make sure you're fine and have everything you need."

"You surprise me sometimes, you know."

"Good." He grinned. "I like keeping you on your toes."

She gave a small, indifferent shrug, but he sensed she was far from indifferent. Vi was a person who liked the unexpected and the thrill that came with it. If Cole let himself, he could become completely enamored with her.

At her house, he gave her some alone time to change into lounging clothes. After twenty minutes, he knocked on her bedroom door.

"How goes it?"

"Come in."

She stood beside the bed, pointing the remote at the small TV atop the dresser and flipping through channels.

A magazine, bottled water and her cell phone occupied the nightstand, and extra pillows were stacked at the head of the bed.

"You aren't lying down," he scolded.

"I will. I just gave Gabe a call to update him."

Cole had assumed he'd be the one to break the news about her scare to the family. Well, she had worked for Gabe much longer than for Cole or Josh. Old habits were hard to break.

"What are you hungry for?" he asked. "Figured I'd stop at the café for takeout. It's chicken-fried steak night."

"Sounds perfect. With a side salad, please. I'll pay you back."

"I am not taking your money, and I'm not arguing with you about it."

"I feel guilty enough as it is, accepting a paycheck when I'm home…sick."

"We've been through this already," he insisted.

"I know. Doesn't change my feelings."

"Can they be changed?"

"Not about money and accepting charity."

He moved closer to her. "I was thinking of me. What are your feelings on *that* subject?"

Her gaze locked with his. "It depends."

"I'm counting on them changing."

"Why?" she asked earnestly.

"Because I'm not the guy you think I am, Vi. Make that the guy you thought I was."

"And what kind of guy are you, Cole? I really want to know."

"My word is sacred. I keep my promises. My moral compass mostly points north. I make mistakes, but not the same one twice."

She smiled, showing off those amazing dimples.

He leaned in. How could he not? Her green eyes widened, then softened. Her lips parted ever so slightly. It would be easy to kiss her, and for a second he considered doing precisely that.

Instead, he took her by the arm and eased her onto the mattress, first sitting and then lying down. He picked up one of the extra pillows and positioned it beneath her feet, elevating her legs as per Dr. Medina's orders.

When Vi was comfortably prone, TV remote in her hand, he bent, brushed her hair off her face and delivered a chaste peck to her forehead. "See you soon. No getting up. I mean it, Vi."

She nodded. He thought that maybe, once again, he'd taken her by surprise, and grinned. This was getting to be fun.

At the door, she called his name, halting him. "I'm glad you're staying. For the next few days," she added, as if he might have misunderstood.

Pleasure coursed through him. She was glad, and it was enough, for now.

VIOLET WOKE EARLY, which wasn't unusual. She rose by five o'clock most days. Before then, if necessary.

Having overnight guests…now that was different and unsettling. No one, not even Raquel or Cara, had slept at her house in all the years since her divorce—other than Cole, and he'd done so twice in the past two-and-a-half months. One big difference. Last night he'd slept on the living room couch and not in her bed.

She stood in the doorway that connected the kitchen to the living room, watching him slumber. With a start, she realized she'd missed him. Missed his body lying next to her during the night and wrapped around her when they woke. Most of all, she'd missed the low, seductive rumble of his voice in her ear as he wished her good morning.

How was that possible? They'd been together only one night. A total of twelve hours from the time he'd walked into the bar to when he'd left the next morning. They'd been intimate a mere eight. Yet it felt much longer. Days. Weeks. Months. Their connection had been instant and powerful, once they'd stopped denying their mutual attraction and yielded to it.

Just enough light filtered in through the slit in the drapes for her to discern his form on the couch in the gray of early dawn. His blanket lay on the floor beside him. He'd slept in his underwear—boxer briefs. They were dark in color and smoking hot. During their night together, he'd slept in the nude, as had Violet.

Resisting the sudden rush of memories, she pulled her bathrobe tighter, annoyed at her erratically beating heart.

What nonsense. She was hardly some love-struck teenager crushing on a boy in her class. And she certainly wasn't falling for Cole Dempsey. It was one thing to like him. Even lust after him in secret. But love?

Violet hated being vulnerable, which was exactly what being in love did to a person. Her baby came first. Having feelings for Cole, loving him, would only be setting herself up for pain and sorrow. He'd eventually leave, returning to the rodeo circuit, and possibly not come back. She'd been through that before with Denny; he'd left for different reasons, but still, he'd left. She didn't care for a second go-round, thank you very much.

She might have stood there indefinitely if not for Diamond Girl. The small, buff colored Siamese sauntered in from the living room, meowing loudly.

"Shh."

The cat rubbed lovingly against her leg, purring loudly.

Violet bent to pet her, catching sight of Stripes, her tabby, maintaining a safe distance. He was a reformed feral she'd found living behind a convenience store, and brought home. He adored her. Everyone else, not so much, as evidenced by the way he glared at Cole.

Diamond Girl resumed meowing.

"All right already," Violet whispered. "I'll feed you."

She'd started to retreat to the kitchen when Cole suddenly stirred. Ignoring the demands of her feline charges, she sneaked another peek at him.

Sweet heavens, he was beautiful. Tanned, smooth skin, abundantly muscled limbs, a toned torso that stretched long and lean. One arm was draped casually behind his head, and his feet hung over the edge of the couch. Really, he was much too big for it.

How could he have gotten any decent rest like that? She'd hardly slept herself, her mind racing a mile a minute and refusing to shut down. He'd been mere feet away, down the hall and around the corner. Had he struggled like her, tossing and turning while obsessing about the other person in the house?

Looking at him, peacefully asleep, she doubted it and, to her annoyance, she felt a sharp stab of disappointment. Why should she be the only one to suffer?

"You're supposed to be resting."

His voice startled her, and she involuntarily jerked. He sat up, taking his sweet time and not bothering to cover himself. Hair the color of tarnished gold stuck out at funny angles, somehow making him look sexy rather than silly.

Damn, there went her heart again. *Bump, skip, bump.*

"I needed coffee." She held up the mug in her hand.

"Caffeine's bad for the baby."

"It's decaf." He'd been listening to Dr. Medina. Violet

went from being disappointed to being pleased. He did care. "Can I fix you a cup?"

"Have any regular? Decaf's not enough to start my motor revving in the morning."

After looking at him for a full ten minutes, her motor was purring louder than Diamond Girl's. "Sure. Coming right up."

"I'll make it. You go back to bed."

"Cole." She crossed her arms over her middle. "I'm allowed to be on my feet an hour a day."

"How long have you been awake?"

"Are you timing me?"

"If that's what it takes."

His concern was…adorable. Oh, God. How could she continue resisting him? Especially in such close proximity.

Afraid her voice might betray her, she cleared her throat. "Are you hungry? I have oatmeal muffins to go along with the coffee. Packaged, not homemade."

"My favorite kind." He stood.

Her mouth went dry at the sight of his boxer briefs riding low on his hips, and her fingers resumed clutching the fabric of her bathrobe collar. He obviously didn't have a self-conscious bone in his body.

"I'll get your coffee." She spun on her heels to avoid giving herself away, if she hadn't done so already. The next two nights with him promised to be just as long and restless as the last one.

When Cole joined her in the kitchen, she was relieved to see he'd slipped on his jeans and a T-shirt. With clothes on, she had a much better chance of being able to face him, to sit across from him at the table, without losing her thinly held composure.

She placed a mug in front of him, coffee black, the way he liked it. They'd shared enough breakfasts at the ranch house for her to be familiar with his tastes. The morning after their night together, she'd been in such a hurry to get him out of the house, she hadn't offered him so much as a glass of water.

The muffins, three of them, fit nicely on a paper plate. They went onto the table, along with a tub of butter, two glasses of orange juice, Violet's prenatal vitamin and a couple bananas. She didn't care much for the fruit, but she'd been bothered by nightly leg cramps lately and read somewhere that the potassium in bananas helped.

"You're too good to me," he said, helping himself to a muffin and the knife. He broke the muffin in two and slathered a huge glob of butter onto each half.

Thankfully, conversation flowed easily over breakfast, perhaps because it centered on work and not on the two of them. She almost wished they weren't getting along. Her choices would be easier then and she could insist on Raquel or Cara staying with her rather than Cole.

They were just finishing when Violet's cell phone went off, playing a familiar ring tone. She groaned, scrubbing a cheek with her hand.

"Someone you'd rather avoid?" Cole dusted off the crumbs that clung to his shirt. He'd wolfed down a banana and two of the muffins like a starving man.

"It's my mother." For a moment, Violet considered not answering, but at the last second, she got up and went to the counter where she'd left her phone. She swiped the screen and put the phone to her ear. "Morning, Mom."

"Honey, tell me," her mother blurted in a rush. "What's wrong?"

"Nothing. Why?"

"Are you sure? Some woman just called to confirm your doctor's appointment. When I told her you didn't live here, she apologized and hung up. Are you sick?"

Violet shook her head in confusion. She'd listed her mother's number in the event of an emergency, not as a primary contact. Someone at the doctor's office must have made a mistake.

"I'm not sick, Mom. I'm—" Violet's phone beeped, signaling she had another call. Checking the screen, she saw it was Dr. Medina's office. "Let me phone you right back. It's the doctor on the other line."

"I'm not going anywhere. Don't you dare hang up on me."

"Fine." Violet placed her mother on hold, then took the call from the doctor. After confirming her follow-up appointment and correcting the phone number mix-up, she returned to her mother. "Sorry about that."

"You still haven't told me what's wrong."

Violet caught Cole's eye. He remained seated at the table. In fact, he appeared permanently rooted in the chair. Didn't he have to be at the ranch soon? She supposed, as one of the owners, he could set his own hours. But there were a hundred pregnant cows left to check, and that would take most of the day, even with help.

"Don't you have work?" she mouthed.

"It'll wait," he mouthed back.

Drat. She either ended this call with her mother, asked Cole to give her some privacy, left the kitchen and sought refuge in her bedroom, or bit the bullet and leveled with her mother in front of him. Well, at least he'd see firsthand how persistent her parents could be.

"It's a follow-up exam, Mom."

"Follow up to what?"

In the background, she heard her mother drawing on an electronic cigarette. Violet wasn't sure she approved of the practice, but quitting smoking was hard for her mom, who'd tried countless times in the past. The electronic cigarette seemed to be helping with her efforts.

"I wasn't sure if and when I was going to tell you."

"Violet!" her mother practically screeched.

She hesitated, bolstered her courage and said, "I'm pregnant."

Her mother audibly gasped. "Is it Denny's?"

"No! Why would you think that?"

"You haven't mentioned seeing anyone."

"Because I'm not."

"You must be. That's how these things usually work. Unless… Violet! Don't tell me you went to one of those sperm clinics." She all but choked on the last two words. "You're young, your biological clock can't possibly be ticking."

"I didn't go to a clinic, Mom."

"Who is he, then?"

No inquiries about the baby or about Violet's health. How far along she was. How she felt. If she was happy. Then again, what did she expect? Her parents, both of them, had always been completely and totally self-absorbed. All that mattered to her mother was whether or not the father was someone she considered acceptable.

Violet held the phone to her chest. "She wants to know who the father is. Should I tell her?"

"That's your business." A twinkle lit Cole's blue eyes. "But if you're asking do I mind, the answer's no."

She returned to the phone. "It's Cole Dempsey."

Her mother sucked in a breath. Or perhaps she'd taken another drag on her electronic cigarette. It was hard to tell. "August Dempsey's son?"

"Yes."

"The one you don't like?"

"That's not true."

Violet proceeded to fill her mother in on a few of the details, during which Cole wore a none-too-subtle smile. If she didn't find him so damn sexy, he'd irritate her no end.

"You will keep me posted," her mother said when Violet finished describing yesterday's scare and the doctor's cautiously optimistic prognosis.

"I will."

"I'll tell your father tonight when he calls. He got a suite at Manor House, in case you're interested." She took another drag. "He'll want to come see you. Probably this weekend. Make certain you're doing all right."

Violet bit back a groan. "That's not necessary, Mom. In fact, I insist."

"I'll come, too. I can help with the house. Take care of you."

That was a joke if ever Violet heard one. It had always been the other way around. "I'm fine." She sent Cole a fleeting glance. "I have help."

His brows shot up, but he didn't comment.

"We'll talk more about this later. I have to run. Tennis with the girls, then a board of directors luncheon for the community arts committee."

What, Violet wondered, would her mother do post-divorce? All her activities were directly or indirectly related to her role as wife to one of the city's more prominent financial brokers.

Violet disconnected, then laid the phone on the counter, her hand instinctively going to her belly.

"Bad news?" Cole asked.

"My parents want to come for a visit. Soon. This weekend."

He lifted his bare foot and, placing it on the bottom rung, pushed her chair out. "Sit."

Not exactly gentlemanly, but very much Cole and, okay, she admitted it, appealing.

Doing as he'd instructed, she sat and let out a long breath.

"I take it you don't want your parents to visit."

"They love me, don't get me wrong, and will be happy about the baby. But they have an agenda, they always do. Even before they started divorce proceedings, they tried their best to get me to take sides. It's one of the reasons I dropped out of college my freshman year and hit the road. What kid wants to be constantly put in the middle?"

"That's not very fair of them."

"They aren't terrible people. Not really. They used to hate my job and my lifestyle, but they've come around. Mostly because they liked your father and Raquel. It didn't hurt that your dad was one of the valley's leading citizens. Position in the community matters to my parents. Makes telling people what I do a little easier. According to my mom, I'm a bovine management specialist employed at a premier cattle operation."

Cole would be described as one of the owners. Not— gasp!—a professional cowboy or rodeo champion.

He sat back, and Violet sensed his disapproval.

"It's complicated," she said, feeling suddenly defensive.

"You don't have to explain complicated family dynamics to me. I'm an expert. At least tell me they're happy about the baby."

"Mom sounded glad. I think Dad will be, too." Violet paused. "They'll probably want me to move back to Seattle."

Something flickered in Cole's eyes, an emotion hard to define. "Will you?"

"Absolutely not. Mustang Valley is my home." She

didn't add that he was here, too, since his stay continued to remain undecided.

Cole got up and made himself another cup of coffee, appearing at ease in her kitchen despite it being only his second time there.

"I was supposed to graduate with a degree in finance like my father," she said, surprising herself with the admission.

Cole returned to the table. "Me, too, with a degree in business management. My mother went crazy when I started rodeoing. Having one son competing professionally was bad enough. To have two?" He chuckled.

"She probably didn't expect you to marry a junior executive on the career fast track like my parents expected of me."

"You got me there."

Violet absently swept muffin crumbs into a small pile with the side of her hand. "They're still hoping. They tried to lure me home after my divorce."

"I'm glad they didn't."

She gazed at him, curious as to his meaning. "I can already feel the screws tightening, and they haven't even arrived yet."

"You don't have to move," Cole said. "There's nothing wrong with being a livestock foreman."

"I love what I do. Your father didn't just give me a job when I showed up on his doorstep, he ignited a passion and gave me a purpose. I'll always be grateful."

"Was it him who taught you to ride?"

Violet noted the curiosity in Cole's expression and found it interesting. He didn't talk much about August. He certainly didn't ask questions. Not of her. This was a first.

"I started riding when I was six. My parents sent me to summer camp and horseback riding was my favorite program. When I got home, I asked for lessons. They refused, and I literally pitched a fit for weeks until they relented. English pleasure, hunter-jumper and dressage, naturally. My mother didn't approve of Western riding. I never sat in a Western saddle until your dad hired me. He said good riders are born, not made, and it didn't matter what style I first learned."

"And a horse is a horse."

She smiled. "He said that, too."

Cole looked away. "I don't remember much about him."

"A shame. He was a good person. Kind. Generous. I was flat broke when I arrived in Mustang Valley."

"Your parents refused to help you just because you dropped out of college?"

"Oh, they'd have given me money. On the condition I come home. I refused. I was on my way to Rio Verde when my car ran out of gas. I had no idea what to do, other than cry, when your dad drove by. He stopped, put a couple gallons of gas in my tank from the spare can he carried in the back of his truck, handed me twenty dollars and directions to the ranch. I spent the night parked behind the café. The next morning I drove to Dos Estrellas. He hired me on the spot even though I didn't know the first thing about cattle. I learned fast, though, and worked my way up. He promoted me to livestock foreman right before he got sick."

"It's a nice story, but you're not going to alter my opinion of him." Cole's voice hardened. "He turned his back on Josh and me, and on our mother."

"I'm not trying to change your mind, Cole. I may, however, try to open your heart."

After a moment, his sexy grin appeared in full force, potent as ever. "Now, that's different, and something you just might accomplish if you're talking about us."

Chapter Seven

Cole passed the plastic water gun though the rails of the round pen and into the hands of his niece, Kimberly. "Don't fire this until I tell you to, okay?" He leveled a finger at her.

Giggling, she promptly pointed the water gun at him, squeezed the trigger and soaked the front of his jeans. "Ba, ba, ba."

"You're supposed to spray the horse. Not me."

Her answer was to soak him a second time.

What was he thinking, expecting a fourteen-month-old toddler to follow directions? His nephew would probably be equally unreliable.

"Are you ready?" he asked the boy.

"I ready, Uncle Cole." Nathan also stood outside the round pen, not far from his sister. Only he held a different type of plastic gun. This one fired foam darts.

Cole had been recruited to babysit while his brother went to meet with his attorney. Josh's ex-wife was pushing for increased visitation, probably in retaliation against Josh and Cara moving in together. At least, that was Cole's opinion. Even though Josh gave his ex the benefit of the doubt, and treated her more than fairly, he'd scheduled the appointment to discuss his legal options.

Raquel would have watched the kids, but she'd come

down with a nasty cold. Cara was busy, frantically laboring dawn to dusk in preparation for the upcoming launch of the equine therapy program. That had left Cole. He was okay with the task as long as he could call Vi periodically.

After three days, she was still doing fine. That didn't stop him from worrying.

Since training wild mustangs wasn't an option today, not with two young tagalongs, he'd decided to work with one of the horses Cara had selected for the therapy program instead.

This particular mare was called Mama because she'd once fostered an orphaned colt. Her gentle and nurturing nature extended to small children, as well. Training her had been about the easiest job Cole had taken on. As one last test of Mama's reliability, he was putting her through an obstacle course consisting of objects to navigate around and over, along with surprises designed to scare or startle her. Hence the water and foam dart guns.

If she reacted calmly, then she'd be cleared for use in the program. If not, then either her training would continue or she'd be returned to the herd and another horse selected. Cole's niece and nephew would be the determining factor.

Cole had faith in Mama.

"All right." He picked up her lead rope. Up till then, the horse had been standing patiently. A good start. "Wait until I say go," he told the kids.

Kimberly squeezed the trigger again, wetting Cole's boots. He sighed and gave up.

Mama didn't so much as flinch when he led her past the pole with the flag fluttering in the wind, the scarecrow dressed as an old lady and the boom box playing loud rap music. She merely snorted and shook her head when struck with six foam darts. By the time Cole led her past Kimberly, the little girl had lost interest in the water gun and dropped it on the ground.

Cole reached through the rails and retrieved the gun, then sprayed Mama. She looked away as if bored. Cole deemed the test to be a rousing success and gave the mare a well-deserved pat. "Good job. You're hired."

"Cara!" Nathan sprinted off in the direction of his father's girlfriend, Kimberly right behind him. "I help Uncle Cole," he announced proudly.

"I see." She swooped up both children and, balancing one in each arm, approached the round pen, her long black hair blowing in the breeze. "Looks like things are going well."

"Mama's amazing." The dusty brown horse followed Cole to the railing and stopped when he did, ears pricked forward and tail swishing. "Completely bombproof."

"I'm glad. That gives us four horses in total. Enough to start, though I'd like to add two more over the summer. I'll take Mama's picture later and upload it to the website."

Cara had discovered that potential students—they were never referred to as customers or clients—and their parents enjoyed seeing the riding stock on the website and often requested a certain horse. The fact that all the horses were once wild mustangs only added to their appeal.

Nathan and Kimberly objected when Cara put them down.

"You're much too big for me to hold the both of you," she said, letting her arms go limp in an exaggerated motion. "My muscles are tired."

Kimberly hung on to Cara's leg, and she stroked the child's head. Cole knew Cara was careful about her relationship with the kids, determined not to replace their mother, only to be their devoted friend and caregiver. That hadn't stopped the kids from falling in love with her or her with them.

"How have you been?" she asked Cole.

"All right."

"I see your truck's still in the shop."

"Tell me about it." He winced.

"What's wrong? Are they taking too long?"

"Yeah, and I'm going to have a gaping hole in my wallet where my money used to be."

"Guess that'll teach you not to haul ass through the desert."

"Everyone's a critic."

The kids resumed playing with their toys, finding delight in shooting water and foam darts at each other. Cole kept an eye on them, planning on intervening if the playing went too far and became rough. He wasn't entirely irresponsible.

"You look tired." Cara studied him critically. "Was the couch at Violet's not comfortable?"

Vi had made it clear to everyone at the ranch that she and Cole weren't sleeping together. He'd done the same, understanding it was important to her.

"The couch was fine." The lumpy cushions weren't what kept him awake for those three nights. Rather, it was the idea of Vi snuggled warm in her bed. Alone. He'd have liked to be snuggled under those covers with her. "I have a lot going on."

Cara arched a brow. "Understandable. You're going to become a father soon. Which reminds me, how is Violet doing?"

"Good."

"No...relapse?"

He shook his head. "Nothing."

"What a relief."

Cara's smile was sincere and kind, demonstrating what a truly big heart she possessed. A few years ago, she'd lost her young son in a tragic accident. That she was able to accept Josh's kids in her life and wish nothing but the best for others was a true testament to her character. It also showed how much she loved Cole's brother.

For that, Cole fully supported her relationship with Josh. But he was less accepting of interference from her when it came to him and Vi, if that was indeed the reason for their conversation.

"You're going to be a good father, Cole. I'm sure of it."

"I'm not like Josh."

"You're more like him than you think. You're also a lot like your father."

That was the second time in less than a week he'd been accused of resembling his father. Vi had made a similar remark.

"Those are fighting words." Cole was only half teasing.

"He was a good man."

Cole grumbled to himself. What was it with everyone praising his father lately?

"He'd be tickled pink to know he was having another grandchild."

Cole tensed and would have walked away if not for the kids. "Can we talk about something else? What other horses did you have in mind for the therapy program?"

"I get that you're angry. August did hurt your mother."

"Not just my mother." Cole stared off into the distance, recalling an event from long ago he'd prefer to forget. "I came here once when I was seventeen. I'd had a fight with my mom, one of many, and decided maybe everything she'd said about my father wasn't true. Rode a bus over six hundred and fifty miles, then hitched a ride from the bus stop to the ranch."

"I didn't know."

"I'm sure good ole Dad didn't advertise it." Cole cut off Cara when she would have said more. "Because he sent me away. Took one look at me and told me to go home."

"That must have been hard on you."

"When Vi landed in Mustang Valley, broke and needing help, he took her in. Not me. His own son."

"Holding on to your anger and resentment won't change a thing, and it certainly won't make you happy."

"You can stop with the lecture, Cara."

"I didn't mean to give you one." She bent, kissed each of the kids on the cheek and then straightened. "Violet needs you. Now and after the baby's born. I just hope you won't let your feelings for your father prevent you from doing right by her and staying in Mustang Valley."

"And now you're telling me what to do."

"I'm sorry. I've overstepped. It's just I care about the both of you very much and want you to be happy."

Her words stayed with Cole long after she'd left.

Lugging Kimberly in one arm and with Nathan trailing behind him, he returned Mama to her stall in the area reserved for therapy horses. Josh was due back shortly, and not a minute too soon. Cole needed to get ready for the arrival of Vi's parents.

They'd refused to listen to her protests and were due this afternoon, insisting on meeting the father of their first grandchild. Cole's guess was they were coming to size him up or, if what Vi said was true and they wanted her to move back to Seattle, determine how much of a fight, if any, Cole would put up.

A big one, he decided. Vi wanted to stay here. That was good enough for him.

"Daddy!" Nathan hollered, when Josh's truck pulled around the side of the stables.

Cole delivered the kids safely into their father's hands, then hurried to his room in the ranch house, where he cleaned up and changed into fresh clothes. Hopping into one of the ranch trucks, he drove to Vi's house, glad to see there wasn't a rental car in the driveway. He'd beaten her parents.

When she didn't immediately answer the bell, he pushed the door open. Yes, he was taking liberties, but he felt justified. What if something had happened? She might be in distress and unable to come.

"Vi? Where are you?" When she didn't respond, he hurried to her bedroom. Without hesitation, he went in. "Vi?" The room was empty.

All at once, she stepped out of the adjoining bathroom, wearing only a towel, and came to a sudden halt. "Jeeze, Cole."

"Sorry." He should have turned away, except he couldn't. His feet were frozen in place.

She was stunning. Wet hair clung to her neck and shoulders. A pair of killer legs peeked out from beneath the terry cloth. Small, shapely hands clutched the front of the towel, holding it together. Enormous green eyes focused on him.

"Do you mind?" She glowered at him when he didn't move. "Cole!"

"Sure, sure." He was amazed he could speak, what with his jaw hanging open.

The next instant, the doorbell rang. It could only be Vi's parents. Their timing was impeccable.

"I'll get the door." Cole left, but not before giving her another long, lingering look.

It was clear from the expressions on her parents' faces that they weren't at all happy to see him instead of their daughter.

"Where's Vi?" her father demanded.

Cole refused to be intimidated. "Hello, Mr. and Mrs. Hathaway. It's nice to meet you."

VIOLET SHOULD HAVE figured on her parents arriving early. It was a tactic her father frequently employed in business, with the intent to rattle the other individual and gain an advantage. It irked Violet. She was neither an adversary nor a business associate. She was his daughter.

Unfortunately for all of them, the qualities that made Edgar Hathaway enormously successful in his job didn't serve him well in his personal life, and tended to alienate those closest to him. If not, he wouldn't now be facing the end of his thirty-one-year marriage and residing four states away from his daughter.

"Hi, Mom. Dad." Violet breezed into the living room, where her parents waited with Cole, a lead weight residing in the pit of her stomach. She hadn't needed her father to unsettle her. Cole had accomplished that easily enough.

What were the chances of him walking in on her at the same moment her parents arrived on her doorstep? She'd dressed as fast as possible, choosing capri pants and a blouse instead of jeans solely because it would make her parents happy. Seeing approval in their expressions, she was glad she'd taken the time.

Cole's expression did more than gladden her. A sliver of pleasure wound through her at his appreciative stare, more intense than when he'd discovered her wearing only a towel. Come to think of it, he hadn't ever seen her in anything but jeans, either.

Wrong as it might be, she enjoyed his reaction. Violet didn't always feel like a girl. Cole succeeded that in spades.

"I take it everyone has met," she said with as much cheer as she could muster, giving first her father and then her mother a kiss and hug.

"Yes, we have." Her mom held her tighter and longer than usual. Violet smelled the faint minty odor from her flavored electronic cigarette.

"Good," she said. The momentary rush of affection and sentimentality was unexpected. Could their divorce be affecting her more than Violet thought?

"Let me have a look at you." Her mother studied her for several seconds. "You're positively radiant," she gushed.

"Pretty as ever," her father interjected, his eyes shining as they roamed her face. "I'm surprised this young man hasn't run off with you. If he doesn't wise up soon, some other guy is going to steal you away."

"Dad!" Did he have to say that?

She'd attempted to explain her relationship with Cole to her mother when they'd spoken yesterday, along with their reasons for postponing certain decisions. Some of those reasons were becoming less important as her pregnancy advanced, but Cole still hadn't said anything, and Violet refused to bring up the subject. Her patience was beginning to wear thin.

Cole smiled, not appearing the least affected by her father's remark. So much for him disarming Cole.

"Vi's definitely a catch," Cole remarked.

A catch? Dated and chauvinistic remark aside, if she was such a catch, why hadn't he asked her out so that they might get to know each other better?

Annoyed at both men and determined not to let it show, she asked, "Mom, Dad, can I get you something to drink? I have diet soda in the fridge or iced tea."

"Your father thought we might drive into Scottsdale for dinner at that seafood restaurant he likes."

"Why don't we have dinner at the café? It's closer, and the food is good."

"Come on, Vi." Her father put an arm around her shoulders and squeezed. "This is a celebration. Your mother and I are going to be grandparents."

She rolled her eyes at his use of her childhood nickname. Now Cole would think it was perfectly acceptable.

In the end, Violet agreed to the seafood restaurant, if only to keep the peace. Her father insisted on driving and taking the rental car, a luxury sedan. She slid into the backseat, assuming Cole would join her. Instead, her mother climbed in.

Violet wasn't at all comfortable watching the backs of her father's and Cole's heads, and strained to hear their conversation over her mother's chatter. Finding it impossible, she scolded herself for worrying too much and concentrated on her mom.

"Did the doctor have good news for you at your follow-up visit?"

"All is well. She gave me another ultrasound. I made copies of the image if you want one."

"Of course I do." Her mother reached across the seat and patted Violet's knee. "How's your morning sickness?"

"Easing up a bit."

Violet relaxed. Her mother's enthusiasm, and her father's, too, such as it was, pleased her. They might not approve of all the decisions she'd made in her life, but they truly did want a grandchild and would love the baby with all their hearts.

She heard the tail end of something Cole said to her father. It sounded as if they were discussing the weather, except that made no sense. Her dad couldn't care less about anything to do with cattle ranching. She supposed he was simply trying to get along with Cole. He'd made an effort with Denny, too.

"I spoke to your grandmothers," her mother said. "Both

of them. And your aunt Sylvia. They're thrilled and insist on invitations to the shower.

"Mom, I wish you'd wait awhile longer before telling people."

"Oh, darling. You're having a baby. You can't expect me to keep quiet." Her mother went on, not hearing a thing Violet said. "Naturally, you'll have to fly to Seattle for the shower. I was thinking—"

"I'm not going to Seattle."

"You can't expect your grandmothers to fly here. At their ages?"

Cole glanced at Violet over his shoulder, his expression questioning.

"We'll talk about this later, Mom." She gnawed on her lower lip in an effort to remain calm.

This passive-aggressive push-pull was as typical for her mother as unnerving people was for her father. Both of them went after what they wanted with little regard for others.

Violet distracted herself by concentrating on her father and Cole, who, of all things, *were* talking about the weather. Her gut screamed that her father was up to something, and she hoped Cole didn't walk into any traps.

When they arrived at the restaurant—finally—it was to learn they already had a reservation, thanks to a call her father had made earlier. She should have known he'd get his way. He always did. The hostess escorted them to a table facing a huge picture window, through which could be seen a dazzling view of the desert at sunset.

Cole requested a beer. Her mother's frown was fleeting but unmistakable. In her opinion, beer was a blue-collar beverage. She'd selected an expensive red wine for herself, while Violet's father ordered a single malt scotch. Naturally.

"Do you have sparkling water?" Violet asked the waitress when it was her turn.

Small talk continued while they enjoyed the view and perused the menus. Violet couldn't shake the feeling that all was not well despite appearances to the contrary. Her parents smiled a bit too brightly and talked a little too loud.

"I understand you're a rodeo champion." Violet's mother addressed Cole. "How exciting."

"Champion is a stretch, ma'am."

"Call me Julia. Please."

"Thank you."

"But you have won rodeos?" She tilted her head inquisitively.

Violet cringed. Why did her mother always have to push?

Cole, on the other hand, didn't seem to mind the line of questioning. "I can claim a few of the gold buckles on display at my grandparents' home."

"Gold buckles? For belts?"

"It's a coveted award in rodeo, Mom," Violet interrupted.

"Ah. How nice."

"You attend college, young man?" her father asked.

"Mostly the school of hard knocks, of which I've had my share."

Her father cleared his throat.

By some miracle, Violet managed to keep her mouth shut for the most part during the remainder of the dinner, though it wasn't easy. Not soon enough for her, their server swooped in to clear the plates. Violet was eyeing the door when her mother insisted on dessert.

"You must try the cheesecake. It's their signature dish."

While they waited for dessert, the moment Violet had been dreading most arrived. Her father cornered Cole.

"If you don't mind me asking, what are your plans regarding my daughter?"

"Dad!" Violet's hands flew to her face.

"I'm not sure what you mean by plans, sir," Cole said evenly.

"Are you getting married?"

This was going from bad to worse. "Dad, it's none of your business."

To his credit, Cole remained unfazed. "We haven't decided yet."

Lines of displeasure creased her father's brow. "Why not? Don't you think it's the right thing to do?"

Violet beat Cole to the punch. "I'm not ready. For marriage."

"Need I remind you that you're having a baby?"

"No, Dad, you don't. I'm pretty aware of it every morning when I toss my cookies."

"No reason to be crass," her mother admonished, then changed tactics. "You must understand that we're concerned."

"A man takes responsibility for his child," her father said.

"That's enough." Violet placed her hands on the table as if to rise. What Cole said next stopped her.

"I agree, sir, and, I assure you, I will take responsibility. However, I would think at this time you'd be more concerned about Vi's health than her marital status. She did just have a recent scare. Stress isn't good for her or the baby."

Violet swallowed a gasp. Not many people stood up to her father.

"You're right." Her mother patted her hand. "Violet's health is what matters the most."

Their server returned, carrying dessert. Violet couldn't

have been more grateful for the interruption. When the check came, Cole tried to pay. Her father wouldn't hear of it and practically snatched the black tablet holding the bill out of Cole's hands.

"My treat," he insisted.

Cole's jaw moved very little when he spoke. "Thank you, sir."

Another tactic of her father's. Engage the other person in a power struggle and win. He practically gloated.

She'd never admired Cole more than tonight. "Thank you for not losing your temper," she murmered, as he pulled her chair out.

"No reason to."

Further talking was impossible as Violet's mother came over and linked arms with her. Violet suspected the move was intentional.

"You don't mind if I steal her from you? We haven't seen her in almost a year, and I miss her terribly."

Cole graciously stepped aside.

Once again, they drove with the men in front, the women in back.

"Cole seems like a nice young man," her mother said.

"He is. Very nice. You and Dad, not so nice."

"Don't be angry. We just want to be sure."

"Of what?"

"Well, you know."

Violet gritted her teeth. "No, Mom, I don't know."

"That he's right for you."

"And if you're not sure? What then? Are you going to forbid me from seeing him?"

"We'll talk more tomorrow."

"He's my child's father, whether you like it or not."

Her mother removed her electronic cigarette from her purse, probably in preparation for the moment they arrived at Violet's house, where she could stand outside and enjoy it. "Let's not ruin the evening."

Ruin the evening? As if it wasn't ruined already. Violet considered arguing. Only she wouldn't. Not in front of Cole.

Ten years away from home, and nothing had changed. Was it any wonder she refused to move back to Seattle?

Chapter Eight

Cole refused to abandon Vi and leave her to fend for herself in this pool of sharks.

Okay, sharks was a gross exaggeration. Despite her parents' inexcusable behavior, they genuinely loved their daughter. But they were so intent on taking a piece out of each other, they failed to notice how much their actions affected the people around them. Especially Vi.

When the four of them arrived at her house, Cole made sure to accompany her inside. Julia turned to him, a sweet-as-pie smile on her face, her hand extended for a shake.

"It was a pleasure to meet you. I hope to see you again before we leave."

Somehow, he doubted it. On both counts.

Before he could answer, Vi cut in. "Cole's not leaving."

Julia blinked in surprise. "He's not?"

Damn straight.

"Not yet," Vi said. "It's still early."

"Oh." Julia's hand fell limply to her side, but she recovered quickly and stepped in front of Cole. "I was hoping your father and I could visit with you for a while. It's been so long."

"You can," Vi said. "We'll all visit."

On a different day, Cole might have let himself enjoy this small victory. Tonight, however, Vi's motives probably had more to do with using him as a buffer between her and her parents than desiring his company.

Not that he blamed her. He hadn't endured such an awkward and uncomfortable dinner since last Thanksgiving, when both fractions of the Dempseys were joined together for the first time. To compare Vi's family to the days following his father's death was saying a lot.

In the living room, everyone located a place to sit. Vi's Siamese greeted them with a loud meow. She reached down to pet it, and when the cat persisted meowing, headed to the kitchen, presumably to refill the food dish.

Cole stayed behind with her parents. Squaring his shoulders, he readied himself for whatever came next.

Edgar leaned back in Vi's recliner. "With beef prices on the rise these days, cattle ranching must be quite profitable."

"Prices are going up, but trust me, it's not because ranchers are raking in the money."

"Someone is."

Cole ventured a guess at what Vi's father was implying. "If you're questioning my ability to support my child—"

"Now, now. No need to get defensive."

"I'm not. Just being honest."

"In that case," Julia interjected, "let me ask this. Can you afford the kind of upbringing he or she deserves?"

"What kind of upbringing is that?" Cole asked. He might not be rich, but he wasn't on the brink of poverty, either. Rodeoing had provided him with a decent living. And if his brothers bought out his share of the ranch, he'd have more than enough money to support his child for years.

"Violet's child shouldn't lack for anything."

He faced Julia. "Excuse me, ma'am, but no child should."

Edgar cleared his throat yet again. "Vi tells me your

FREE Merchandise is 'in the Cards' for you!

Dear Reader,

We're giving away FREE MERCHANDISE!

Seriously, we'd like to reward you for reading this novel by giving you **FREE MERCHANDISE** worth over $20 retail. And no purchase is necessary!

You see the Jack of Hearts sticker above? Paste that sticker in the box on the Free Merchandise Voucher inside. Return the Voucher promptly...and we'll send you valuable Free Merchandise!

Thanks again for reading one of our novels—and enjoy your Free Merchandise with our compliments!

Pam Powers

Pam Powers

P.S. Look inside to see what Free Merchandise is **"in the cards"** for you!

grandparents own a large horse ranch in California and that you plan on running it when you retire from rodeo."

"I may. I'm not sure."

Cole and Josh weren't the only ones in line to inherit a share of their grandparents' ranch. They had grown up with four cousins, as well.

Plus for all Cole knew, his grandparents could decide to sell their ranch after they retired and spend the money traveling the world. They'd certainly earned it.

"What aren't you sure of?" Vi asked, entering the room.

Edgar squirmed.

Cole couldn't explain why, but he came to the older man's rescue. "Your father and I were discussing cattle prices."

"I can't believe you still have those cats," Julia said, when Vi sat on the couch beside her. "Tell me you'll find homes for them before the baby's born."

"I love my cats."

"They're dangerous to newborn babies."

"Mom, that's an old wives' tale."

"I think you should ask your doctor."

Cole wasn't fooled. Julia had purposely steered the conversation away from Edgar's questioning. He found that very interesting. For two people whose marriage was supposedly over, they appeared to look out for each other.

Vi managed some of her own conversation steering. "Anyone in the mood for coffee?"

"I'd rather have a scotch," her father said.

"No, Edgar." Julia might have been scolding a recalcitrant child. "You have to drive us home."

Home being the resort in Scottsdale.

"Don't harp on me."

She exhaled sharply and turned her back on him.

"Doesn't matter, Dad," Vi said. "I don't have any scotch."

"What about whiskey?" he grumped.

"You aren't going to make me drive," Vi's mother scolded. "I can't see well at night."

"I'd be happy to take you to the resort, Mrs. Hathaway," Cole said.

"I told you to call me Julia."

Edgar narrowed his gaze at Cole. "Are you implying I've had too much to drink, young man?"

"Not at all, sir. I'm merely offering to drive Julia."

"I'll take care of my wife."

"Mom, Dad." Vi visibly struggled to control her temper. "Please don't argue."

Cole stood, went over to her and held out his hand. "Let me help you with that coffee."

She gave him an appreciative smile, as if he had, in fact, rescued her from a school of sharks. In the kitchen, he stayed close to her side and would have liked to kiss her if the timing wasn't off.

"Hang in there," he said.

"They're impossible."

"They mean well."

She laughed. "You can't seriously be defending them. Wasn't my father asking you about your ability to support the baby when I walked in?"

"I might want to know the same thing if I was in his shoes."

"You wouldn't be that rude."

"Who's to say what I'd do?" Cole reached into the cupboard for mugs while Vi readied the coffeemaker.

"I just wish they were more supportive. Isn't it enough that I'm happy with where I live and what I do?"

"Don't look at me. My mom would do cartwheels in the street if I came home and went to work for my grandparents."

That made her smile. "I'm not getting rid of my cats."

As if in answer, the tabby stepped out from beneath the table and blinked at Cole with marginally less antagonism.

"Cut your parents some slack. At least they care, unlike my father." Cole put an arm around Vi's shoulders. "Besides, they'll be gone by Monday."

Whatever her parents were whispering about, they quieted the moment Cole and Vi returned to the living room, each of them holding two steaming mugs of coffee. Vi set her pair on the coffee table, while Cole delivered a mug to her father, receiving a gruff "Thank you" for his efforts.

They'd barely had a second sip when Julia broached the subject of Vi moving back to Seattle.

"It only makes sense," she argued. "Won't you please consider it? The house is huge. You and the baby would have plenty of room. And since you and Cole aren't getting married…" She let the statement dangle.

Cole had stated his position at dinner. He wasn't about to repeat himself.

"I'm staying in Mustang Valley," Vi said firmly, to his vast relief.

"Sweetheart, I can't bear the thought of my first and only grandchild growing up without me nearby."

"You could move here after the divorce."

Julia let out a startled gasp.

Edgar burst into laughter. "She's got you there, Julia. Throwing a wrench into your perfectly devised scheme."

"I have no idea what you're talking about."

Edgar turned to Vi. "She wants you and the baby to move in with her because she thinks that will force me to give her the house in the settlement."

Julia scowled. "Nonsense."

"We both know I'm right." Edgar sat up straighter, his laughter fading. "We're selling the house."

"But I love it."

"You'll find another one you love. Smaller. More affordable."

"You're only doing this to get back at me."

"Quit being melodramatic."

Cole sensed Vi's trembling and saw the tears filling her eyes. He couldn't take any more, and obviously, neither could she.

"If you don't stop arguing," he said, "you're going to have to leave. It's important Vi avoid stress."

Edgar stiffened. "You can't be serious."

"I'm very serious, sir."

"How dare you talk to us like that." Julia's heavily made up eyes widened. "We're Violet's parents."

"Excuse me, ma'am, but you don't exactly act like parents."

"That's enough," Edgar barked.

"I agree," Cole stated. "More than enough."

Julia gasped so hard she started coughing. Edgar had apparently been stunned into silence.

Cole continued with as much congeniality as he could muster. "Edgar, Vi says you're an avid golfer. You'll need an early tee-off time. It's hot by noon this time of year."

As expected, Vi's parents didn't stay much longer. After Julia's attempts to pressure her daughter failed, she decided she was tired. Cole doubted they were done, merely retreating temporarily so they could start fresh tomorrow.

He let Vi walk them to their car while he remained inside. She returned five minutes later.

She shut the front door, leaned her back against it and let her shoulders slump. "I know I shouldn't say this about my parents, but I'm so glad this night is over."

"I'll leave now, too." Cole moved slowly in her direction. "You really do need your rest."

It wasn't his intention to kiss her. But she didn't move from the door, and lifted her gaze to study him. Cole was a lot of things, being made of stone not one of them.

Her green eyes glistened, drawing him in. He couldn't resist, not that he wanted to. He could, however, exercise restraint.

Dipping his head, he brushed his lips across hers. Briefly. He didn't dare risk more. Even so, the sensation was incredible. Enough to weaken his control if he weren't careful.

"Good night, Vi. See you tomorrow." He reached around her for the doorknob.

She stayed his hand by taking it in hers. "Don't go, Cole."

"Are you sure that's a good idea?"

"I am. You were sweet tonight, and my parents were awful."

Ah. That was it. "You don't owe me."

"Which isn't the reason I want you to stay."

"What is?"

"You and I have made a baby together. But the truth is, we don't know each other very well."

"True." Cole was tempted to kiss her again. And again.

She smiled flirtatiously, causing his control to go from weak to practically nonexistent. No woman had ever affected him like Vi.

"I think we should get better acquainted."

He was in complete agreement.

"Look at the moon." Vi pointed to a corner of the star-filled sky. "It's beautiful." When Cole didn't respond, she glanced over her shoulder at him.

He stood there, immobile.

"What's wrong?" she asked.

He looked around her back yard. "You have patio furniture."

"Yes." She laughed softly. "Lots of people do. It goes with the patio."

"I had no idea." When she sat, he did, too. "Adirondack chairs." He slapped the wide wooden armrests. "I like them. They remind me of the beach."

"See? We're learning new things about each other already. I have patio furniture, and you like Adirondack chairs. Now, look at the moon."

He did, and nodded appreciatively at the nearly full sphere hanging as if suspended from invisible wires. A mild breeze sifted past them from the east. Vi had donned a lightweight cotton shawl, her sundress not providing enough protection against the falling temperature.

"You been to the beach a lot?" she asked.

"My mom used to take Josh and me to Ocean Beach every summer when we were kids. We'd rent a condo for two weeks. Had the time of our lives, next to rodeoing.

"It sounds fun."

"For a while, I think I was thirteen, I wanted to be a surfer."

Violet tried to imagine Cole on a surfboard, his blond hair long and wavy, wearing colorful swim trunks and saying things like "dude" or "gnarly." She burst out laughing.

"What's so funny?" he asked.

"You liked surfing?"

"I *loved* it. But I wasn't very good."

"I'm surprised, considering how athletic you are."

"Rodeoing requires a different skill set."

Another cool breeze wandered by. Violet took a moment to enjoy it. "This is nice."

He reached across the space to capture her hand in his. "This is better."

Yes, it was. Strong male fingers linked with her much smaller ones. The sight caused a stirring inside her that could only be called romantic.

She considered demanding the return of her hand, despite flirting with him earlier. She and Cole had yet to define their relationship or settle on a direction. Granted, he had initiated the conversation. Twice. But she'd insisted they postpone until her pregnancy reached that important first milestone, and then was frustrated when he didn't broach the subject again.

In a few days, she'd pass that milestone. Perhaps it wouldn't be tempting fate too terribly much if she and Cole made one or two small decisions.

"Do you think you might make Mustang Valley your home base?"

There, that wasn't difficult. It was also completely reasonable. Nothing like *Should we get married? Should we discuss visitation or joint custody?* Or, *How do you really feel about me?*

"I do," he said. "Now that you're certain you won't be moving to Seattle."

"I was never moving to Seattle. That's my mother's idea."

It was his turn to laugh. "Strange as this sounds, I like your parents."

She gaped at him. "You're joking."

"They're interesting people. And challenging."

"Two words that describe them to a tee. But you forgot frustrating and infuriating."

"Loving a parent isn't always easy, trust me. My mom's also a difficult person. Bitter and angry all the time. For a lot of years, I blamed Dad. Took me a while to realize she just plain likes being unhappy. And she had more to do with Dad staying away than she claims. I'm pretty sure she'd have taken his head off if he so much as came within a hundred miles of us."

"He really was a wonderful man. I can't imagine he didn't want to be a father to you."

"I concede I might not have been entirely fair to him, but he could have found a way to see us if he'd really wanted to."

"That goes both ways."

Cole seemed about to say something, closed his mouth, then started again. "You're right. There's no good excuse for me not coming to see Dad when he was dying. I'll regret that the rest of my life."

Violet didn't push the point. It was enough that Cole had started to come around. It would be impossible for her to truly care for a man who didn't admit his mistakes.

"I'd like to meet your mother one day," she said. "Have you told her about the baby?" Funny, it hadn't occurred to Violet before now to ask.

"Not yet. I will. Soon."

"Do you think she'll be glad?"

"She adores Josh's kids. Spoils them rotten. I'm pretty sure she'll be excited." Cole leaned his head back and groaned. "She'll probably want to come out when the baby's born, if not sooner. Consider this fair warning."

"I thought she refused to return to Mustang Valley."

"She'll make an exception for her grandchildren."

Violet smiled. "Great."

He groaned again. "You say that now."

"Personally, I hope she's an involved grandparent. I want to surround my child—*our* child—with lots of family and friends. Raquel, Gabe and your dad were like that with me. I love being included even if I'm not technically a Dempsey." Though by having Cole's baby, she felt more like a member of the family than ever before.

"You're a pretty special person, Violet Hathaway." He squeezed her fingers.

His sincerity touched a place deep inside her.

For the next several minutes, they stargazed in silence, their emotional bond quietly growing. Violet had many more questions to ask, but was unsure where to start. Suddenly, an idea came to her.

"Let's play a game."

Cole glanced at her. "What kind of game?"

"I think you'll find it enlightening."

He shook his head. "What am I getting myself into?"

She ignored him and explained the rules. "Each of us will take a turn voicing one doubt we have. About us, our relationship, the future, whatever. Then we'll discuss it. List the pros and cons. Hopefully, find some common ground or learn something new about each other."

"I'm assuming you've played this before?"

"Kind of. Yes." As teenagers, she and her friends had engaged in a version of the game, though it had been more about obstacles they'd faced with the boys they liked and the boys liking them back.

Cole considered her suggestion for a few moments before relenting with obvious reluctance. "You first."

"But—"

"The game was your idea."

She could hardly argue that and picked a relatively straightforward concern.

"I'm worried about us being able to work together, now that we're in a personal relationship, and not let our feelings get in the way."

His expression brightened. "We have a personal relationship? That's great—and here I thought I'd have to woo you."

She matched his light tone, trying not to read too much

into his remark. "Not that. The baby. We'll be coparenting, which could affect our business relationship. What if we disagree on something? That could carry over to the job."

"Only if Josh and Gabe don't buy me out."

Her stomach sank. "Then you're definitely leaving."

"If I don't go back to rodeoing I'm not sure how I can earn enough money to support the baby. Which, for the record, is one of *my* concerns."

"The ranch should start turning a profit, sooner or later. Then you can draw a salary."

"I doubt we'll see much profit this year. Possibly next spring, when we can sell off more of the calves." He didn't sound optimistic, causing her stomach to sink lower.

"You could always do something else to earn income."

"Like what? Rodeoing and ranching are all I know, and I'm not good at ranching yet."

"Horse training? You love it. And it's something you can do to supplement your income while ranching."

"So is rodeoing."

"Without leaving," she clarified.

He crinkled his brow. "I'm not sure there's enough money in part-time horse training. Mustang Valley is a small town."

"Are you kidding? Mustang Valley is a great place for a horse trainer. Especially with Cara's therapy program taking off like gangbusters. You told me yourself she needs two more horses over the next few months."

"Cara doesn't pay me for training."

"Maybe she should."

The lines in his brow deepened. "I wouldn't feel right about that."

"Fine. Then partner with Powell's riding stables. Their clients are always looking for well-trained horses. And what about roping or cutting horse clinics? Powell Ranch has a riding arena. You could pay them a percentage of your revenues in exchange for using their facilities."

He stared at her. "Thought about this much?"

"Not at all. I'm just… There are plenty of opportunities if you think creatively."

"Maybe." He shrugged. "I do like training horses."

"See?"

"You sound like you want me to stay."

Was that a trace of hope she detected in his voice? "You're my baby's father. Of course I want you to stay."

He searched her face. "Is that the only reason?"

Before she quite knew it, she uttered a soft, "No."

That seemed to satisfy him. "All right."

"You'll do it? Explore the possibilities?"

"Yeah." He didn't sound enthused.

Vi, however, was. Very enthused. "Good."

"There's still the problem of mixing business with pleasure."

The way he said "pleasure" caused a spark of desire to ignite in her. "I said *personal*."

"Oh, right." His grin went from playful to sexy.

Violet almost moaned as the spark burst into a bright flame. She was definitely getting in way over her head.

"I think, if we set some ground rules and abide by them, we can both act professionally," she stated. "Gabe and Reese are managing well enough working together and they're engaged."

"Her term as trustee of my dad's estate will come to an end, hopefully in the next six months. Then there won't be a conflict."

"True."

When Violet turned and met Cole's glance, something in his eyes had changed. "We could always get married," he said hesitantly.

She tried not to react. "Is that what you want?"

"I'm…not against it."

Hardly a sweep-a-lady-off-her-feet proposal, if it even was a proposal.

Violet swallowed, thinking carefully before responding. "Let's wait until I've reached my second trimester."

"Okay, what's next?"

Was it her imagination, or did Cole seem a bit relieved?

Suddenly, she didn't want to play the game anymore. "We can stop now. I said one or two concerns each, and we've done that."

"But I don't want to stop. This is fun."

"Fine," she said irritably, then blurted, "Will you resent me for tying you down when you'd rather be on the road?"

He sat back in his chair. "That's a really good question."

"Which means you might."

"These past seven months have been the longest I've stayed in once place since I left home at eighteen. In some ways, it's been hard. I won't lie. In other ways, it hasn't."

"Not being hard isn't the same as being easy."

"Ranching is different from rodeo. But I've adjusted better than I thought."

"What changed you?"

"I ran into this pretty little gal at the Poco Dinero Bar one night three months ago, and she took me home with her."

"Cole. I'm not joking."

"Neither am I. Gabe and Raquel, they've had something to do with it, for sure. But it's you, more than anyone, who've caused me to change. For the better, I hope." His gaze raked over her, lingering when it found her face.

Oh, boy. If she and Cole continued like this, she wouldn't be able to hold on to her soaring heart.

She had to be careful, she reminded herself. Soaring hearts were always in danger of crashing and breaking.

"I think we should head in," she suggested.

"It is getting late."

Not even a small protest? She didn't know whether to be annoyed or glad.

Inside, Cole retrieved his cowboy hat and truck key from the kitchen table where he'd left them. She assumed she'd walk him to the door. Instead, he pulled her into his arms.

"I'm going to kiss you good-night, Vi. Pucker up."

No romantic buildup? No preamble? No seeking her permission with soft caresses and tender words?

"And if I say no?"

He grinned confidently. "Will you?"

Why in heaven's name was she hesitating? Only one choice made sense. Send him home. Right now. This instant.

"Last chance," he teased.

Every cell in her brain urged her to listen to reason. Not make a mistake she could ill afford.

Instead, she looped her arms around his neck and pulled his mouth down to meet hers. "If anyone's going to do the kissing around here, it'll be me."

Chapter Nine

"I'm not playing any games now." Cole broke off their kiss before the last shred of his finely held control snapped. "We either stop and I go home…"

"Or? If we don't?" She smiled up at him.

Was she serious? He couldn't tell. Maybe it was time he closed his eyes and took a leap of faith.

"Then I stay and we see where this leads. Because after that kiss, you have to know how much I want you."

She wanted him, too. He wasn't so befuddled by lust he didn't recognize her response for what it was. Desire. Need. Hunger.

"Maybe I require a little more coaxing." Her mouth curved seductively.

Another kiss? He could do that. Take possession of her mouth, wrap her tight in his arms, mold her sweet body to his and let her experience the full extent of his longing. The last minutes had been exquisite. Well worth repeating.

"Is it safe?" He gave up thinking of a polite way to say it. "Did Dr. Medina give you the green light at your last follow-up?"

"She did."

"But you're not ready."

"I'm not sure. I mean, I'm not confident, even if we were to be careful."

"I understand." He tried to mask his disappointment. "I would never do anything to hurt the baby."

She gave him an entreating look. "You could still stay. Spend the night with me. We'd just…we wouldn't…"

"We wouldn't make love."

"I know. Not the same." She glanced away as if embarrassed.

"I'd love to spend the night with you, Vi. I can't think of anything I'd rather do. And I won't take advantage of you."

He'd be tempted—he was only human, after all. But he'd respect her wishes. The baby was their priority.

"I'm glad. I wasn't ready for the night to end." She stood on tiptoes and kissed his cheek. "Give me a few minutes to change, if you don't mind."

"Not at all."

He went to the hall bathroom and, locating a tube of toothpaste in the medicine cabinet, did what he could to get ready for bed. Staring at himself in the mirror over the sink, he shrugged out of his shirt.

Wait. On second thought, Vi might jump to the wrong conclusion. He put the shirt back on but left it hanging open.

Uncertain what to do next, Cole returned to the living room and sat on the couch. A minute later, he stood and paced.

"Sorry I took so long."

Hearing her voice, he spun and felt his mouth go bone dry.

She wore a silky, dark maroon nightgown with narrow straps and a hem that fell slightly above her knees. He'd seen more suggestive sleepwear but never anyone sexier than Vi. She very nearly robbed him of his breath.

"Come on." She inclined her head in the direction of the hall and, he assumed—or hoped—the bedroom.

He followed her, hesitating at the threshold. She'd turned down the bedspread. One of the cats, the tabby, lay in the middle. It scampered away at the sight of him, darting between his legs and disappearing down the hall.

"We scared Stripes," Vi said. "Poor little guy."

Personally, Cole was glad to see the competition thinned. He'd much prefer Vi's attention focused solely on him.

She climbed beneath the covers. When Cole hesitated, she patted the mattress beside her in invitation.

He swallowed, his throat still dry. "You're gorgeous."

"You're exaggerating, but I appreciate the compliment. Been a while since someone gave me one."

He still didn't move.

"Something wrong, Cole?"

"What the hell," he muttered under his breath, before removing his shirt, peeling off his socks, unbuckling his belt and stepping out of his jeans. He walked to the bed wearing only his boxer briefs.

He sat on the edge of the mattress, taking his time as much for her as for himself. "I know we don't have all the answers yet. Far from it. But we have the most important ones. I care about you, Vi." He possibly felt more for her than caring, but wasn't quite ready to tell her. "We're committed to raising our child together to the best of our abilities, and we're both going to stay in Mustang Valley. It's a start, enough to build on."

"I don't disagree."

He threw her earlier words back at her. "Which isn't the same as agreeing."

She looked up at him. "You're right—we're both committed to our child. And I care about you, too. You impressed me tonight, you know."

"With my talents at dinner conversation, you mean?"

She smiled. "When you came to my defense. It meant

a lot to me. The only one who's ever stood up to my parents before was…"

"Let me guess. My dad."

"I did say you were more like him than you think."

Reclining on the pillows, he was careful not to let his arm or leg brush hers. Any contact, and he might not be able to stop. "I really hope not. I intend to be a better father."

She shifted, and he struggled not to stare. It was difficult. The subtle changes in her body were evident beneath the satiny fabric of her nightgown. Fuller breasts, slight swelling of her belly, rounder hips.

There would be little sleep for him tonight.

"Good night, Cole." She reached over and switched off the light.

He was immediately thrown back to three months earlier and the first time he'd slept with Vi. There'd been no awkwardness like tonight, and they'd lain entwined like familiar lovers.

"Good night, Vi." He kissed her chastely on the lips.

"This is nice." She edged closer.

"Yeah, nice." Actually, it was pure torment. In hindsight, he probably should have gone home.

All at once, he felt her hand on his chest, and every muscle in his body tensed. She threw a leg over his. He gritted his teeth. She nestled her face in the crook of his neck. He suppressed a groan.

She had to be aware of what she was doing to him. She wasn't oblivious.

"Vi."

"Yes?" Her hand crept lower.

"What are you doing?"

"Having second thoughts."

"Don't take this the wrong way. I'd like nothing better

than to make love to you. But I won't do something we'll regret in the morning. We've been down that road before."

Her hand traveled another inch. And another. "Who says we'll have regrets?"

"What about the baby? I won't take any chances."

"We have plenty of options," she said silkily. "We just have to use our imaginations."

Had he heard her correctly? Possibly not, as a roar filled his ears.

"What are you saying?"

In answer, she wrapped her fingers around him.

His body reacted with a mind of its own, growing instantly hard.

"Nice." She began stroking him, slowly at first, then faster.

Cole gulped air, convinced if he didn't get sufficient oxygen, he'd pass out.

"Kiss me," she said.

He turned his head, their mouths a hairbreadth apart. "This isn't going to be all about me, just so you know. I intend on making you very, very happy."

She made a low, throaty sound that pushed him to the boundary of his limits. "I'm counting on it."

They spent a night like none other, exploring each other's bodies with their hands and mouths and bringing each other intense pleasure, made greater by deepening feelings.

When they were spent and completely satisfied, they snuggled. Vi told Cole about burning all the parenting magazines after her divorce. He told her about his first rodeo win at fifteen.

Before long, she fell sound asleep. Cole didn't move. He didn't ever want to leave her bed. Come morning, he'd have no choice. For now, however, he'd relish the sensation of her curled beside him, and consider a future that didn't terrify him quite as much as it had before.

THE FIRST TIME Violet had woken up in bed with Cole beside her, she'd panicked. On this morning, she hunkered deeper beneath the covers, sighing with contentment when his arm snaked around her waist and anchored her to his side. Not that she'd been more than an inch away all night.

Things were far from resolved. Some might say the two of them were heading into much more dangerous waters than before. But for the moment, Violet was content. Cole, too, she suspected.

"Morning," he whispered in her ear.

"It's still early. Go back to sleep."

The numbers on her digital alarm clock indicated it was 6:17 a.m. Late for a workday.

"I can't. We have a Cattlemen's Association meeting this morning." Cole groaned and stretched.

She sneaked a peek at his long-limbed body and remembered. How many men would be that considerate, that patient? Willing to please a woman with less conventional—but no less satisfying—lovemaking?

She wouldn't have guessed it of Cole. Not when she'd first met the then-surly cowboy. He had indeed changed. Or not. Maybe the man she knew today was the one who'd always been there, just buried beneath a thick layer of hurt and resentment.

She thought back to the time last fall he'd sold off his horses to save the sick steers. That said a lot about his character. A man who put family first and who kept his promises—she could love a man like that. She certainly wouldn't want any other kind for the father of her child.

"I'd better get up." He threw off the spread.

"If you want, I'll make you some coffee while you shower."

Sitting up on the side of the bed, he grinned over at her. "I'd like that. Actually, what I'd really like is to shower with you." He stared at her naked body and sucked in air through his teeth. "But I'd better wait and shower at home, where I can change into clean clothes."

His comment reminded her that him spending the night had, once again, been spur-of-the-moment. Neither of them were prepared.

"I'll take the coffee, though," he added. "If the offer still stands."

"It does." She dashed across the room, very aware of him watching her as she grabbed her robe and donned it. Her nightgown hung crookedly on the bedpost, where it had landed last night in her haste to undress.

"I'd like to see you later," he said, while she poured his coffee into a plastic travel mug. He'd dressed in his clothes from yesterday and stood at the kitchen counter.

"Mom and I made plans to go to brunch this morning while Dad golfs. Then, later, they're coming to the ranch. Raquel invited them to dinner."

"That was nice of her."

"Actually, she and August always got along with my parents. And before you ask, I have no idea why. They couldn't have been more different."

"Does this mean you're announcing the baby to the rest of the world?"

Violet hadn't forgotten that the only people who knew of her pregnancy were Cole, his brothers, her parents and those relations her mother had told.

"Are you okay with that?" she asked.

"It's entirely up to you."

With her first pregnancy, she'd informed anyone who

remained still long enough to listen. For two whole weeks. Then she'd miscarried and all those people kindly offered their condolences. It had been a nightmare.

The second time, she'd been a bit more cautious, telling only family and several very close friends. Fewer condolences that time. She'd insisted on saying nothing about her third pregnancy. The only reason her parents found out was because Denny accidently let it slip one day when Julia happened to call.

Violet dreaded the prospect of facing everyone should she lose this baby. But come tomorrow, she'd be twelve weeks along—a minor miracle.

"I guess I could make an announcement. Though I wasn't planning on doing it at dinner. Maybe I'll say something to Raquel afterward."

"Will your mom stay quiet till then?"

"Probably not." Violet pictured the scene, feeling a combination of nervousness and excitement. "Raquel will be surprised."

"That you're pregnant or that I'm the father?"

"You being the father is going to give her a heart attack."

Cole smiled, the kind of smile that made Violet's insides turn to mush. "She loves kids. She considers Josh's two her grandchildren. She'll love ours, too."

Would *he*? Violet cared much more about his feelings for their child than Raquel's.

"I'm sure she will," Violet agreed.

Cole came up behind her and put his arms around her waist, then nuzzled her cheek. She closed her eyes. If only their circumstances were simpler. Didn't she deserve a happy outcome after all she'd been through?

"I'll see you at dinner," he said.

He kissed her cheek, then kissed her again, much more

passionately, before leaving. Violet allowed herself to believe, for a few precious minutes, that this was the beginning of something special.

She'd just finished putting a load of laundry in the washing machine when there was a knock on her door. She felt her heart leap, thinking Cole might have returned. But that made no sense; he was on his way to the meeting.

Her parents? Not likely. Mom enjoyed sleeping in, and Dad didn't miss his golf game unless there was an emergency.

All those thoughts and others occupied Violet's mind as she hurried to the front door. A glance through the peephole caused her to break into a grin, and she opened the door to her visitor.

"Raquel! Hi. What brings you here?"

In answer, the older woman held up a basket. "It's not too early, I hope. I see you aren't dressed."

"Not at all. Come in."

"I brought you some leftovers."

The word *leftover* was a joke. Raquel didn't know how to make food in small quantities. There was always extra. Violet had been the lucky recipient of the other woman's bounty on many occasions, mostly when she was sick.

"Thanks. You didn't have to."

They went to the kitchen, where Raquel deposited her basket on the counter. "It's nothing much. Just some of this and that."

The basket actually contained a small feast, including tortillas, rice, salsa, two desserts, a container of green chili pork and braised cabbage.

"Wow," Violet gushed. "This is more than I can eat in a week."

"I thought you could use some food around the house. Your father's always liked my cooking."

"Thank you for having us to dinner tonight."

"My pleasure. I always enjoy seeing your parents. We're eating at six, but come earlier. And be sure to bring Cole."

Violet nearly choked. "Cole?"

"Oh." Raquel looked chagrined. "My mistake. I thought you two were seeing each other."

"He, ah, we…"

"Yes?"

Violet wasn't ready yet. "It's complicated."

"I'm sorry." Raquel touched her shoulder soothingly. "I was obviously out of line. I didn't realize your pregnancy was a secret."

"You know?" She gasped. "Did Gabe tell you?"

"No. We just assumed."

"We?" Violet struggled to keep her voice level. "Who's we and what did you assume?"

"Cara, Reese and me. We've noticed you've been sick a lot lately. I mentioned to them I'd seen you like this before. When you and Denny were married."

"I see."

"Are you? Pregnant?"

"I was going to tell you tonight. My parents only learned about it last week."

Raquel pulled Violet into an affectionate hug. "I'm so happy for you. And Cole."

"What made you think he's the father?"

"Well, Cara saw the two of you heading out of town with your parents last night. She said the truck Cole borrowed wasn't back at six this morning when she arrived at the ranch. She put two and two together."

"Great. I've been found out because of a truck."

Raquel laughed, the sound warm and rich. "We were already thinking it was Cole. We're not blind. He's been following you around like a stray dog for weeks."

"We work together."

"Oh, please." Raquel dismissed that with groan. "I'm not blind. You should see how he looks at you."

"How?" Violet was almost afraid to ask.

"Like a man head over heels."

Was it possible? Did she dare hope?

"Not that it's any of my business," Raquel said, "and please tell me if I'm overstepping, but I thought the feeling was mutual. I've seen the way you look at him, too."

Overstepping? That was a hoot. Raquel considered everyone at Dos Estrellas family, and their actions entirely her business. It was quite often annoying as much as it was endearing.

"I care about him." There was no sense lying, because Raquel would see right through her.

"You're afraid he'll leave."

"He says he's going to make Mustang Valley his home base."

"But you want more. A commitment."

"My child deserves a full-time father."

Raquel took Violet outside to the back patio and the same chairs she and Cole had sat in the previous night. Pointing to the nearest one, the other woman said, "Sit."

Violet did, slumping like a recalcitrant child. "I suppose you're going to tell me my expectations are unreasonable."

"Hardly. The exact opposite." A note of sadness crept into Raquel's voice. "I think you should fight for Cole. Unless you don't want him."

"I'm not sure what I want."

"I don't believe you."

"I just wish he were…"

"Thrilled about the baby?"

"Yes," Violet reluctantly admitted.

"In his defense, the baby was probably a bit of a shock."

A thought suddenly occurred to Vi, one that sent a ribbon of alarm coursing through her. "You don't think I planned this, do you?"

"Of course not."

"What if Cole does? That could explain his reservations."

"Has he said anything to you?"

"No."

"Then I wouldn't worry about it."

Easy for Raquel to say. Violet wasn't convinced. She'd lost three babies. Cole could think she'd tricked him, used him to get pregnant.

"You could always ask him," Raquel suggested.

"I suppose." And how would she broach the subject?

"Don't let him get away, Violet. Marry him, if he asks you. Let him know that's what you want." Her expression grew sad. "I always regretted never marrying August. It wasn't fair to Gabe. He suffered, growing up in a small town where everyone knew he was born out of wedlock."

The terms Raquel used were old-fashioned; single mothers were common these days and few people would look down on Violet or tease her child as they had Gabe when he was young.

Nonetheless, she couldn't bear the idea that her sweet and innocent baby would suffer in any way.

"But what about love?" she asked Raquel. "My parents have been miserable their entire married lives. I would hate for the same to happen to Cole and me. And he may resent me for tying him down."

"He won't. Trust me."

"There's no guarantee."

The sense of security Violet had felt so strongly this morning was fading as the day progressed, hastened by her conversation with Raquel.

She was having this child with or without Cole, but she'd rather it be with him, for both her and the baby.

After Raquel left, Violet dressed for brunch, unable to quiet her racing thoughts. Was Cole falling for her? If only she could be sure. Better she not leave herself open for hurt and heartbreak.

Chapter Ten

"You ready?" Josh called, rapping on Cole's bedroom door.

"Give me a minute."

Cole quickly fastened his shirt and tucked it in. Next, he threaded his belt through the loops on his jeans, admiring the gold buckle. He'd earned this particular one in Payson on a bull named Damnation. It was his favorite win and the buckle he usually wore.

He recalled that scary ride and how lucky he'd been to walk away uninjured, much less take home first place.

"Those were the days," he mumbled to himself, and grabbed his boots, sitting on the chest at the foot of the bed to put them on.

He'd missed rodeoing when he first came to Dos Estrellas. Not as much now, though he sometimes craved the excitement and the ever changing landscape. Was it Vi, the baby or the ranch that was responsible? Maybe all three.

"Hurry up." Josh rapped on the door again. "We don't want to be late."

"Coming."

Between Vi's parents' visit and spending the night at her house, Cole had forgotten about the Cattlemen's Association meeting until early this morning. His first months here, he'd rigorously avoided the meetings—that had been his late father's life, not his, and Cole had wanted no part of it.

After much arm twisting from both his brothers, he'd relented and agreed to go, discovering the meetings weren't as awful as he'd anticipated. They reminded him a little of the camaraderie he enjoyed with his rodeo buddies. And with him filling in as livestock foreman, it made even more sense for him to attend.

"Let's go," Josh said, the instant Cole entered the kitchen, his hair still wet from the shower and a nick on his chin from a rushed shave. "You don't have time for that," he barked when Cole reached for a coffee mug. "Get some at the diner."

Cole grumbled but obliged. "Where's Gabe?"

"We're meeting him there." They took Josh's pickup, which prompted him to ask, "When's your truck going to be out of the shop?"

"End of the week."

Josh made a sound of disgust. Cole wasn't sure what his brother was more annoyed at, how long the shop was taking with the repairs or the fact that Cole's reckless driving had landed him in this mess.

"How'd the visit with Violet's parents go?" Josh started the engine. The next second, they were off.

"All right."

"You don't sound enthused."

Cole went on to tell Josh about the evening, though he omitted the part about spending the night with Vi. That was between the two of them.

Leaving her this morning had been hard. He'd relished seeing her at her worst, as she put it, finding her mussed hair and ratty old cotton robe incredibly sexy. If not for the Cattlemen's Association meeting, and his fear of someone discovering their unplanned sleepover, wild horses wouldn't have dragged him away.

Apparently, Vi didn't like being separated from him, either. She'd already texted him twice, with Cole breaking into a smile at the sound of his phone beeping. The messages weren't important, mundane really. Not that it mattered. Just like him, she wanted to sustain their connection.

"Doesn't sound like you had a good time," Josh commented.

"I did, actually."

"During dinner or after?"

Cole frowned at the insinuation. "What are you saying?"

"Cara said you weren't at the ranch when she got there at six. But mysteriously appeared by six-forty-five."

Shoot. Cole should have figured out he'd been caught from the stern scowl his brother wore.

"Vi and I talked. We have a lot to work out."

"For eight hours? What did you do the rest of the night?"

"None of your business." Too late, Cole realized he'd given himself and Vi away.

"I hope you know what you're doing. Violet's vulnerable right now. She's been through a lot."

"The last thing I want to do is cause her more grief."

"But you might. She could easily misinterpret your actions."

"My actions?"

Josh braked at the stop sign and shot Cole a heavily weighted glance. "Women put a lot of importance on sex."

"I happen to put a lot of importance on it, too. This wasn't a one-night stand for me."

"It was the first time you spent the night with her." Josh pulled ahead.

"Only because Vi insisted. I'd have gone out with her again."

"Gone out?"

"Don't say it like that."

"My guess, little brother, is that she wants more from you than dating."

Cole didn't appreciate the tone in Josh's voice. Probably because it hit too close to home. He'd been thinking the same thing himself.

He kept quiet after that. Luckily, Josh got the message and shut up. About Vi, anyway.

"Mom called yesterday." he said as they entered town. "Quinn's being released in two days."

"Finally!" Cole grinned. This was the news they'd been waiting months—no, years—to hear. "I bet Aunt Edna and Uncle Spenser are happy."

"Mom says they're planning a big welcome-home party for him. She wants us to come. I told her we probably couldn't make it on such short notice."

"How'd she take it?"

"Not well. She mentioned coming here for a visit."

Cole suppressed a groan. "I don't suppose there's some way one of us could go." By "one of us" he meant Josh.

"I might be able to get away. I'll talk to Cara. Unless you'd rather be the one."

"No way. You go. Having to take three days off to check the cows has gotten me way behind schedule." Cole wasn't lying; he had fallen behind. But he also didn't want to leave Vi, not with their recent big step forward. "I'll visit Quinn in a couple months. That should appease Mom."

Quinn Crenshaw, Cole and Josh's cousin from their mother's side, had lived in the same town as their mutual grandparents. The three boys grew up together and were the best of friends as well as cousins. Three years ago, Quinn had been wrongfully accused of assault, but a lengthy legal process had found him guilty and he was sent to prison.

The family remained steadfast in their support, never believing Quinn had committed the crime and never abandoning him. By sheer luck, a recent discovery had brought new evidence to light that proved his innocence.

Now, Quinn would once again be a free man. Cole wondered how prison had affected his cousin and if being free would restore him to his former easygoing self.

"I was thinking," Josh said. "What if Quinn came here? After he gets settled."

"To Mustang Valley? Why?"

Josh shrugged. "He's going to need a job. Not a lot of places will hire an ex-con."

"He's no con."

"He spent over two years in prison. It won't be easy for him to explain to a prospective employer what's he's been doing all that time."

Cole didn't want to be selfish, but he had to ask, "Can we afford him?"

"Maybe he'd be willing to work for room and board like the rest of us."

"There's a difference. We're the owners. We can't expect anyone else to work for free."

"I want him to know he's welcome."

Cole understood where his brother was coming from. They were both close to Quinn, but Josh more so. Still, there was the matter of money. The ranch was barely making ends meet.

"Have you mentioned it to Gabe?" Cole asked. "He needs to be included in the decision."

"I figured we could bring it up together after the meeting."

Cole shifted uncomfortably in his seat. His brother was moving kind of quickly. "It'll be interesting to hear what he says."

The three brothers' relationship had been tested often these past seven months. The issues, however, had all been centered on the Dempsey family and the ranch. If Quinn came, Cole and Josh would be introducing an outsider whose loyalties would be with them. Gabe might not like that.

The parking lot at the Cowboy Up Café was full, forcing Josh to find a space across the street with all the other latecomers. As the town's one and only diner, the café had hosted the monthly Cattlemen's Association meeting since the organization's inception seventy years ago.

The group, made up mostly of men, occupied almost the entire diner. They were a noisy lot, too, having to converse loudly in order to be heard above the clinking of glassware, clattering of plates, clanging of silverware and each other.

Cole and Josh were greeted by the assistant manager. The shiny, red high-heeled shoes she wore with her black, tight-fitting skirt weren't typical cowgirl attire and garnered plenty of male attention this morning.

"Follow me, guys." Not exactly a hardship.

She smiled prettily at Cole over her shoulder as she guided them on a crooked course to one of the last empty tables. Cole had always found it hard to tell if she was flirting with him or just being friendly. He didn't respond. This time. Admittedly, he had in the past. Before Vi.

"There'll be two more joining us," Cole said.

"Mary Ann will be right over to bring you coffee and take your order." The woman winked at him before sashaying away, drawing a dozen admiring glances in the process.

"She likes you," Josh said.

"It's her job to like everyone."

"You, especially. Does she know about Violet?"

Cole glowered at his brother. He wasn't in the mood for teasing.

Menus at the Cowboy Up were printed on the paper place mats, not that most people needed one. The fare, basic to begin with, rarely changed.

Mary Ann brought them the promised coffee and jotted their orders on a small notepad. While Cole and Josh waited for their food to arrive, they made conversation with several of their nearest neighbors. Beef prices and the weather were two reliable topics, along with the Millers, a longstanding family in the area who were putting their small ranch up for sale.

Before long, Gabe and his future father-in-law, Theo McGraw, arrived, accompanied by a chorus of jovial howdys and hey theres. Stopped by more than one person, they took a full five minutes to reach Cole and Josh's table.

"Good to see the three of you together," Theo remarked. He sat with difficulty, his Parkinson's requiring him to use a cane. "Your father would be proud."

"That's a fact," commented one of the few women present, from the next table over. "You three have done a good job with the ranch and are to be commended."

Her companion chimed in, echoing the sentiment. "Some of us assumed Dos Estrellas was done for sure when ole August died. Glad we were wrong."

Cole felt a surge of pride rise up in him, something he hadn't experienced in a long while. Not since his last big rodeo win. He, Josh and Gabe had pulled together to overcome some pretty difficult challenges. There was more to accomplish, but they'd made remarkable progress.

They were almost finished with breakfast when the meeting started. It typically ran about an hour, and today was no exception. The interaction of the members was interesting and impressive to watch. These people were competitors in the same business, yet they united for the benefit of all.

At the end of the meeting, some of the members quickly cleared out, while others lingered over coffee.

Theo struggled to his feet. "If you don't mind waiting, Gabe, I'd like to speak to Billy Jorgenson over there."

"Go right ahead." The moment Theo left, Gabe said, "I have some good news. Reese was able to convince the cancer treatment center where Dad stayed to settle for considerably less money, but only if we agree to monthly payments." The reduced amount he cited was significantly lower, enough to make the high monthly payments worthwhile. "We can pay off the balance by November."

A year from the time Cole and Josh had arrived at Dos Estrellas. A month before Vi's baby was due.

"Good for Reese," Cole said.

"Good for us," Gabe seconded. "This is the last of Dad's medical bills. I don't want to get ahead of ourselves—a lot depends on how well we do at the fall sale. But there's a chance we may be able to start drawing small salaries by Christmas."

Cole tried to imagine the changes having income would mean for the family. He could possibly quit the rodeo circuit altogether and reside full-time in Mustang Valley rather than returning every few weeks. He'd be able to help Vi and play a larger role in their child's life. With more to offer her, he might actually embrace the prospect of taking their relationship to the next level rather than proposing out of a sense of duty and responsibility.

"If that's the case," Josh said, "and we can draw a salary, I'd like mine to go toward paying someone else."

Josh's remark snapped Cole back to the present.

"Who?" Gabe asked.

"We have a cousin getting out of prison. I'd like to give him a job. And before you say anything, it's not what you think."

Cole watched Gabe closely, observing his reaction while Josh recounted the story of their cousin's arrest, imprisonment and release.

"Quinn's a decent guy," Josh continued. "An honest guy. And he needs a break. I'd like to give it to him."

"And you'd be willing to sacrifice your salary?" Gabe looked doubtful. "What about Cara? Would she go along with it?"

"She would," Josh answered confidently. "And I'm sure Cole would be willing to give up his salary to Quinn, as well."

"Wait a minute." Cole held up a hand. "I never said that."

"He deserves a chance."

"And I have a baby on the way. I'm going to need every dime I can get my hands on. And in case you've forgotten, Vi's only working half days and, once her vacation and sick pay run out, getting half salary. She needs my help."

"I forgot," Josh admitted.

Gabe pushed back from the table. "This whole thing may be academic, as we aren't even sure yet about drawing salaries. First, we pay off Dad's bill. Then we'll consider hiring your cousin. Before then, you two should probably hash it out, since you clearly don't agree." He paused, his voice gathering assurance. "I can tell you this much. If we can't swing the money, there's no way I'll agree to hiring on anyone new."

For a moment, Josh appeared as if he might object. He wisely refrained.

Wisely because, for the first time in the brothers' relationship, Cole supported Gabe over Josh, and that probably wouldn't go down well.

Settling their tab, Cole, Josh and Gabe agreed to meet up at the ranch. Gabe all but insisted that Cole ride with him. And while Cole complied, he was somewhat puzzled.

"What have you got going on today?" Gabe asked, buckling his seat belt.

"Measuring the livestock pond. Then, inspecting the hay. Joey mentioned some of the bales were moldy." When he was through, he'd come home and clean up before Vi and her parents arrived for dinner.

"How's the pond level holding?"

"Good."

"Huh. Borax." Gabe gave a shrug. "Who'd have guessed?"

"Not me."

"Dad had a lot of old-timer tricks he used. That wasn't one of them."

Cole stared out the passenger window, his mind elsewhere. Josh volunteering both their salaries to pay Quinn had annoyed him. Yeah, Quinn needed a break, and Cole would do his part to help him. That was no reason for Josh to give Cole's money away. Money that, quite frankly, they didn't have yet.

Exhaling slowly, he mentally pulled himself together. This wasn't worth getting worked up over. Quinn might not want to come to Mustang Valley. He had a life and family in California he probably didn't want to leave.

"There's something I want to ask you," Gabe said, a funny quality to his voice.

This must be the reason for the ride back together. "What's up?"

Gabe hemmed and hawed for several long seconds. Cole found it amusing and interesting, as his half brother was seldom at a loss for words.

"Must be serious," Cole prompted.

"I've been trying to approach you for the past week, but I couldn't figure out how. Reese is giving me a hard time, accusing me of stalling."

Now he was really curious. "Just spit it out."

Gabe muttered to himself, then said, "Will you be my best man at the wedding?"

Whoa! Not what Cole had been expecting.

"You don't have to say yes."

"No." Cole shook his head.

"You're turning me down?" Gabe appeared genuinely disappointed.

"I'm not."

"Good."

"I'm just surprised. Why me and not Josh?" He was the one who'd always gotten along better with Gabe.

"That's the thing." His half brother relaxed, a slow smile forming. "I like you better than Josh."

"What?"

"I'm kidding." Gabe grew serious. "I thought long and hard about this. I suppose, in a lot of ways, asking Josh to be my best man makes more sense. But it's important to me that you know how much I consider you part of the family. Josh already does, and not because his girlfriend is like a sister to me."

Cole had had no idea Gabe felt like that. None. They were usually at odds, getting into frequent arguments.

"If you still want to leave," Gabe said, "I'm hoping you'll wait until after the wedding, or at least come back for it."

Cole hesitated before responding, Gabe's request affecting him more than he was willing to admit. If he said yes, he'd be making a commitment. Not only to stand up for Gabe. He'd be saying that he, too, considered himself part of the family.

"It would make Reese happy," Gabe added. "And me."

Cole wondered how Vi would want him to answer. He was pretty sure he knew. "I'd be honored to serve as your best man."

"That's great." Gabe laughed as if relieved of a great weight. "I'm going to ask Josh to be one of my groomsmen."

"He'll be glad."

"He's not the only one."

No, he wasn't.

Cole let the good feeling wash over him. It had been quite a day. Full of emotional highs and lows. And there were bound to be more at dinner tonight.

When they reached the ranch, Gabe surprised Cole again. "How 'bout I ride out to the pond with you? If you're in the mood for some company."

"Sure."

They retrieved their horses from the stables and saddled up, tying the animals side by side at the hitching rail outside the tack room.

Gabe gave Hotshot an admiring glance. "He's a fine-looking horse. You've done a quite a job with him. I'm impressed."

"He made it easy." Cole gave the gelding a solid pat on the rump.

"Did you train your other roping horses? The ones you sold last fall?"

"For the most part. They'd been started. I did the finishing."

"You ever train a horse for someone else?"

Cole tightened Hotshot's cinch, slipping two fingers

beneath the strap to ensure it fit snugly but didn't pinch. "I've helped a few friends now and then."

He recalled Vi's comment last night about him training horses for a living.

"Why not give it a try?" Gabe grabbed hold of his reins, put his boot in the stirrup and mounted the pretty little palomino mare. "You could probably make some decent money on the side. If you're interested."

"When would I have the time?" Cole also mounted. Hotshot happily followed the mare down the stable aisle, completely enamored with her.

"You combined training Hotshot with working."

He had, but it had also taken him five months to bring the gelding this far along. Plus he was covering for Vi and would be for months. "Paying clients tend to be in a hurry."

They walked their horses out into the open and headed toward the gate leading to the pastures. Leroy and Joey waved to them from the hay sheds, where they were searching for moldy bales.

Cole should have dropped the subject, but couldn't bring himself to do it. He asked Gabe the same question he'd raised with Vi.

"Do you suppose there's a market in Mustang Valley for a horse trainer?"

"There is, but I can't say precisely how big. You've met the Powells? They're the ones who founded the mustang sanctuary, before Cara took it over."

"A few times."

"Ethan, the younger of the two brothers, is a horse trainer. He works exclusively with their clients at the riding stable."

"I wouldn't want to compete with a friend of Cara's."

"You wouldn't be if you trained mustangs for the folks adopting them. Talk to Cara about it."

"We'll see." Cole wasn't ready to commit.

"You ever heard of Drew Bankston?"

"Who hasn't?"

The former National champion was a well-known roping instructor. He traveled the entire Southwest, and ran clinics twice a year at the Powell Ranch.

"He's retiring at the end of the summer," Gabe said. "The Powells are going to hate losing him. He brings in a lot of revenue for them. For the whole town. Cowboys come from all over the state to participate."

It was impossible to miss the point Gabe was making, which was as subtle as a sledgehammer to the head.

"I'm no instructor," Cole said.

"You ever help friends?"

"A few."

"There you go."

"I don't know the first thing about putting on a roping clinic."

"I'm sure Drew didn't, either, until he tried."

Cole shrugged, not sold on the idea. "He was a National champion with a lot of credentials."

"I've seen you rope. You're good enough to teach others."

"What?" Cole was thrown for a loop. "When did you see me?"

"Three years ago. At the Payson Rodeo. Dad had already been diagnosed, but was feeling good enough to work on some of his bucket-list items. I didn't realize till your first event that he'd tricked me into taking him so he could see you and Josh compete. I didn't say anything, even after I figured out it was you, and neither did he."

Cole was struck dumb. His father had seen him win the gold buckle he wore now. Watched him accept the prize for the biggest win of his life. And all along, Cole had no clue.

"Why didn't you say anything before now?" he finally asked, his hand going to the buckle at his waist.

"Waiting for the right time."

Cole nodded, though he didn't fully understand. "Thanks. I'm glad you did."

"What I said before, I wasn't joking." Gabe gave him a hard stare. "You are good enough to be an instructor."

"Maybe."

"Start small. Cara can help you. She has experience from putting on mustang adoption events. Can't be that much different for a roping clinic. 'Course, that means you'd have to stick around, which isn't what you want, right?"

"Vi and I are trying to decide what's best."

"I assumed as much, seeing as you spent last night with her."

Cole swore softly. "Does everyone know my personal business?"

"Hard to hide anything around here. My mom has eyes in the back of her head. She read me the riot act the first time I stayed overnight with Reese."

"Is that something I have to look forward to at dinner tonight?"

"I'd steer clear of her for a day or two, if I were you."

They reached the first hill and headed their horses up the trail. The pond lay about a mile to the southeast. Cole kept an eye open for any hidden coveys of quail, not wishing for a repeat of the last time, when Hotshot started bucking and nearly threw him. He wasn't in the mood for a repeat performance, not in front of Gabe.

"She'll cut you some slack as long as you treat Violet right."

"That's my intention."

"I hope so." Gabe rode in front of Cole and shot him a

glance over his shoulder. "Because if you don't, my mom isn't the only person you're going to have to watch out for. Violet's more than an employee. I'll personally take a piece of your hide with my bare hands if you hurt her, brother or no brother."

"I wouldn't blame you if you did."

"Good." Cole heard the smile in Gabe's voice. "Glad we understand each other."

They did.

"You going to marry her?"

"We haven't gotten that far."

Gabe reined his horse to a stop and waited for Cole to catch up. He rested his hands on the saddle horn.

"Not that it's my place to tell you what to do, but I hope you'll consider it. For the sake of your kid. I can tell you from personal experience it isn't any fun growing up the son of a man who won't marry your mother."

"I can't marry her. Not yet."

"Why? Don't you care about her?"

"More than I thought possible," Cole said.

"Then propose."

"I will. When I have a job that pays me a decent income. I have to be able to take care of her and the baby."

"You think that makes a difference to her?" Gabe asked.

"It does to me, and the only way I know how to make money is by rodeoing. Vi wants a man who's willing to settle down, and I am, but as long as I stay here, I'm next to broke."

Gabe grunted in disgust. "Money's not everything."

"Yeah, well, without it we might have lost the ranch."

"That baby's coming in about six months, whether you have a decent income or not. You'd better make up your mind about what you're going to do, and fast."

Gabe was wrong. The way Cole saw it, he had less time than that.

Vi wouldn't wait until the last moment. She might return his feelings, but if he didn't step up, be the kind of man she wanted and needed, she'd move on, raising their baby alone, or possibly with another man, if she met someone.

Cole couldn't let that happen. Under any circumstance.

Chapter Eleven

Cole dropped the foot of the scruffy brown burro and straightened, rubbing an annoying ache lodged in the small of his back. It was tension, not bending, that was mostly responsible. There had been a lot of it lately, especially these past few days.

Cole and Vi were spending as much time together as possible, seeing how things went, but once again they had postponed making any kind of decision regarding their future.

Vi wanted to wait for her parents to leave, and he understood her reasons. Julia and Edgar were high maintenance. They required all Vi's attention and left her drained by the end of the evening. Thankfully, there had been no repeat of the first night. Julia and Edgar were playing nice. With Vi, anyway, if not with each other.

Hopefully, things would return to normal after they left this afternoon. But then what? Cole still didn't have anything to offer Vi other than the choice between a fifty-to-sixty-hour-a-week job that paid zero or one that required him to be on the road ten out of every fourteen days.

With a quick jerk, he undid the slipknot tying the burro's lead rope to the fence post and removed the halter.

Cara had recently acquired a trio of wild burros taken during a roundup near Tuba City. She'd asked Cole to take a look at them, evaluate their overall health and dispositions and determine whether or not they were adoptable.

He'd agreed. Cara wasn't an easy person to refuse. Besides, he might need her services if he ever mustered the courage to put on a roping clinic, which at this point appeared unlikely.

Seizing his chance for freedom, the released burro trotted to the opposite corner of the pen, where his buddies had gathered. Like him, they'd suffered the indignity of having their hooves, teeth, ears, legs and hide thoroughly inspected.

The smallest burro, no taller than Cole's waist, opened his mouth and released an ear-piercing hee-haw likely to be heard by neighbors a mile away.

"Nothing wrong with your vocal cords," Cole said as he closed the pen gate.

"Excuse me, are you Cole Dempsey?"

Cole turned and came face-to-face with a man he recognized from the Cattlemen's Association meetings but hadn't officially met. Blake Nolan.

"I'm him." Cole's smile was reserved. "What can I do for you?"

"Gabe said I might find you here."

"And you did." Cole waited, not revealing his surprise. What was his brother thinking? Blake and Reese had once been involved many years ago—he was the father of the daughter she'd given up for adoption at birth. It was Cole's understanding that they didn't get along, although according to Gabe, their animosity had more to do with work. Blake had dealings with the bank where Reese was employed, dealings that sometimes caused friction between them.

Out of respect for his future sister-in-law, Cole had chosen to keep his distance from Blake, at the meetings and around town. Evidently, though, relations weren't as strained between Reese and Blake as portrayed. That, or things were improving. Gabe wouldn't do anything to hurt his future wife.

Blake shifted his weight restlessly from one foot to the other. "I have a question for you."

"I'm listening."

He gave a short, nervous laugh. "This is awkward." When Cole said nothing, he added, "For me, anyway."

"It might be less awkward if you told me what you wanted." Cole meandered over to the ranch truck parked just outside the pen. The tailgate was down, and he dropped the hoof pick he'd been using into a tool caddy. By then, Blake had joined him.

"I have a problem. Gabe suggested you could help."

"Shoot."

"I have two girls," Blake said. "They wanted a horse, so my parents bought them a Welsh pony. Had him shipped from Oregon and paid a small fortune."

"That doesn't sound like a problem."

"He won't let my girls ride him. Throws them every time."

"Ponies can be mean."

"You see, that's the problem. He's sweet. He'll stand there for hours and let the girls brush him and braid his mane and tie ribbons in his tail. Just don't put a saddle on him."

"Get your girls another pony."

"The thing is, they've gone and fallen in love with him." Blake gave a cynical head shake. "It's beyond my understanding."

"Why, might I ask, did Gabe suggest you talk to me?"

"He claims you're a good horse trainer. Next to Ethan Powell, the best in the valley."

Next to Ethan Powell? Really? Cole drew back. So much for brotherly loyalty. "You want me to train your kids' pony?"

"Gabe said you might be interested in taking on some clients."

"I might be." A pony wasn't how Cole had imagined making a name for himself.

"You've done some impressive work with the equine therapy horses. Or so I've heard."

That was more like it. He could live with a reputation training horses for special-needs children.

"I'd have to check with Reese first."

"She won't object."

No? Interesting. "And I'd need to have a look at the pony. Then there's the matter of my rates."

"Which are?"

Cole named an amount he thought reasonable. Less than what he'd charge for training a roping or cutting horse, but not so low he was giving away his services.

"Sounds fair."

"It'd be easier for me if we kept the pony here for, say, thirty days, rather than me coming to your place."

"My girls will be devastated."

"Bring them by. Might help with the training." The invitation was issued before Cole realized what he was saying.

Blake grinned. "That'd be great."

Too late now.

They discussed a number of details before shaking hands and parting ways. Cole watched Blake leave, feeling a bit off-kilter. He'd just agreed to train a pony belonging to a man his family considered less than a friend, if not an outright enemy.

Life was strange sometimes. Then again, the past seven months had involved a series of one strange event after another. Cole was living at his father's ranch, a place he'd sworn to avoid. He'd agreed to be best man at Gabe's wedding, the brother he never counted on meeting, much less liking. He'd fallen for a woman he hadn't given a second glance when he'd first arrived. Most of all, he was about to become a father.

If that wasn't cause to feel off-kilter, he didn't know what was.

Leaning on the side of his truck, he paused and drew in a deep breath, sweat forming on his brow. He didn't often get scared.

Perhaps he'd made one life-altering decision too many, too soon. Agreeing to train Blake Nolan's pony was a commitment. Another tie to the ranch and reason for him to give up a job he loved in exchange for a future filled with uncertainties.

He didn't know if he loved Vi or she him. He felt all tangled up inside, confused one minute and confident the next.

His cell phone rang. He'd been expecting Cara to call, inquiring about the burros, but the ring tone identified the caller as Vi.

"How goes it?" He started to say "sweetie" but something held him back.

"Great. Taking a moment to rest. Mom and Dad just left."

"I thought their flight wasn't until four."

She moaned. "They've decided to stay another few days."

"Okay." Cole wasn't sure how to respond. "Did they say why?"

"Nothing specific. I suspect they want to meet your mom."

"My mom?" Dead silence followed. "Vi?"

He held his phone away, noted the screen showed an open connection and returned the device to his ear. "You there?"

She cleared her throat. "I think I just said something I shouldn't have."

"What's going on?"

"Josh was supposed to call you. Your mom's coming for a visit."

"When?"

"Day after tomorrow."

Anger and frustration pushed at Cole from all sides. He fought the smothering sensation.

"This isn't unexpected," Vi said reasonably. "She has mentioned it before."

"I didn't think it would be this soon." Or that his mother would really return to Mustang Valley, a place that held only bad memories for her. "I'll call you later, after I talk to Josh."

"Cole…"

"Don't worry."

A short while ago he'd spotted Josh's truck parked behind the horse stables. His brother was probably in the apartment, packing boxes. He and Cara had finally found a small house in town to rent, one they could afford on their budget.

Cole climbed the stairs to the apartment landing. Pulling out his phone, he dialed.

"I'm outside," he said, when Josh picked up.

A moment later, the door swung open. "You don't knock anymore?"

"What's this about Mom coming for a visit?"

"Nice to see you, too."

Cole ignored the sarcasm and entered the apartment. "You should have told me before saying yes."

"I didn't say yes or no. She called to say when she'd be arriving. Plane ticket bought. Room at the inn reserved. End of discussion."

Cole started to say more but was cut short. "Hi, Uncle Cole." Nathan bounded over to greet him, brandishing a sheet of paper. "I coloring."

"That's nice." He glanced around, noting the half-full boxes, rolls of bubble wrap and packing tape. "Where's Kimberly?"

"Napping," Josh said. "Which this young man should be doing, too."

"I not tired, Daddy."

Josh sent Cole a look. "Which means the packing is going slow."

Nathan returned to the dining table, where a pile of crayons lay scattered. He climbed onto the chair with a booster seat and resumed creating his masterpiece, oblivious to everything else.

Cole pushed aside several boxes that were blocking the couch and sat, propping his forearms on his knees. "I really wish you'd told me about Mom coming before Vi did."

"She called right after I hung up from Mom. It slipped out."

"Right."

"What's the big deal? So Mom wants to visit the kids and meet Violet. Did you think she'd wait after you told her?"

"Believe me, that's not the reason she's coming."

"Maybe she's ready to make amends." Josh knelt, closed a box and sealed it with packing tape. "We have."

Cole broke into harsh laughter. "You're kidding."

"Okay, then why do you think she's coming?"

"To convince me, if not both of us, to return to California."

Josh contemplated Cole's answer for a moment. "You might be right."

"I am right. Up until Dad died, we were coming home every few weeks. With you and Cara moving into a house and Vi and me having a baby, that's changed."

"Yeah." Josh looked guilty. "I probably shouldn't have told her I'm thinking of proposing to Cara."

"Congratulations, man. But, yeah, you should have waited." Cole let his head drop into his hand. "This is not going to be easy. Vi's parents are staying on so they can meet Mom."

"It gets worse."

Cole lifted his head, dreading what was next.

"Cara mentioned Mom's visit to Raquel, and now she wants to throw a big party."

"Is she crazy?"

"Evidently so."

For any other family, this would be a fun event. For any other family, the hostess wouldn't have cheated with the guest of honor's husband and had a son with him while he was still married.

"Nervous?" Violet came up behind Cole, placed her hands on his shoulders and squeezed.

"Naw."

She could feel the tension flowing through him and knotting his muscles. "Liar."

"I'm not nervous." He cranked his head sideways to look at her, a glint in his dreamy blue eyes. "I'm scared."

"She's your mother, for crying out loud."

"We're going to have this same conversation tomorrow, after you've met her and seen her in action. You'll change your opinion."

Violet gave his shoulders a last squeeze and sat down.

They were at her kitchen table having coffee, bagels and fruit, Violet's attempt at a halfway nutritious and filling breakfast.

More like brunch, she thought, glancing at the clock on the microwave. They'd slept in. Not surprising, considering how late they'd stayed up the night before.

"You love her. You have to love her." Violet smeared cream cheese on a bagel half. She was often at odds with her own parents, but deep down, she loved them dearly.

"I do. Mom may not have made the right decisions when it came to handling her life, or Josh's and mine, and she can hold a grudge like nobody's business. But she did her best to give us a good home and raise us right."

"From what I've seen, she succeeded."

"The wounds my dad inflicted were just too much for her. She couldn't, or wouldn't, recover. It's the reason she never met someone new. She doesn't trust men."

"She is coming here. That says something."

"Or she has a personal agenda."

Violet knew from talking to Cole over the past two days that he questioned his mother's motives.

"Dos Estrellas has changed you and Josh." Violet downed her prenatal vitamins with a glass of milk. "It might change her, too."

"This place isn't magic."

"I disagree." She pressed a hand to her tummy, reveling in the tiny bulge.

"Pardon me if I don't hold my breath."

"Oh, Cole. It's going to be fine."

"My mom, Raquel and Gabe in the same room can't possibly be fine."

"Don't forget my parents."

He groaned. "This party is going to be a disaster."

"Or, the best thing to ever happen to our families. It might clear the air."

"Yeah, kind of like an explosion does."

She laughed, and it dispelled the small case of nerves she hadn't admitted to having. Whatever the day brought, she felt good about her and Cole.

Okay, relatively good. Violet feared she was living a fantasy, one that would come to an end eventually. But she lived it with her eyes wide open.

"Did I keep you up last night?" he asked. "I was pretty restless."

"No." It was her turn to lie. His constant tossing and turning had disturbed her, though she'd tried hard not to let him know. He already had enough on his plate, and she refused to add to it.

Cole had spent the past two nights with her. He didn't assume and would wait until she suggested he stay. She liked that. It showed he respected her. Neither did he initiate sex, leaving that to her, as well. Aware they were getting more deeply involved, with no real plan for their future, she still reached for him the moment they were in bed together.

The sex—no, the lovemaking—was wonderful. Satisfying and exciting. The intimacy was ten times better. If not for Cole's wanderlust, they'd be perfectly suited to one other.

"Have you decided to take on Blake Nolan as a client?" Given the history, Violet had been quite surprised when Cole mentioned the arrangement.

"Yes. For now. Reese insisted she didn't mind. And it's only for thirty days."

One client, one month, a modest fee. Hardly enough to make Cole want to give up rodeoing for horse training.

"When are the Nolans bringing their pony to Dos Estrellas?"

"Tuesday."

"And you're certain you can train him?"

He gave her a pointed look. "I can train a pony."

"Will you ride him?"

"If I have to. Welshes are bigger than Shetlands."

His confidence was appealing and it was warranted. Cole was good at what he did, though a child's mount was hardly a true test of his abilities. The therapy program horses, like Mama, were something else entirely.

Violet hadn't asked if he'd spoken to Cara about referrals from her long list of people who'd adopted mustangs. Vi didn't want to appear pushy.

"What time are we supposed to be at Josh and Cara's?" She rubbed her foot along Cole's calf beneath the table. He'd dressed in his jeans. No shirt. She wore only a robe.

"One. That'll give us an hour before the party starts to introduce you and Cara to Mom, for her to shower Josh's kids with presents, and for Josh and me to assess the situation. Come up with an alternate plan if necessary."

"Alternate plan?"

"If Mom appears to be gunning for a fight."

"With Raquel?"

"With any of us."

Violet stood and carted dirty dishes to the sink. "I still think you're wrong."

"All I can say is you don't know my mother."

What if he was right? No one wanted a scene between Miranda Dempsey and Raquel. Especially not in front of all the guests. In addition to the McGraws, Cara's parents, from Mesa, would be coming, as well.

Violet was sure that Raquel would behave herself. The past was the past and, with August gone, there was no reason to continue feuding. At the very least, she'd be civil. She wouldn't be hosting a dinner party otherwise.

Miranda, however, was an unknown entity. Violet couldn't help but think she'd be reasonable. Possibly, her sons had exaggerated. Did someone really hold a grudge for twenty-five years?

"I can't wait to meet your family," Violet said over the running water. She was rinsing while Cole loaded the dishwater. "Your mother. Grandparents. Your cousin Quinn if he comes."

Cole leaned in and kissed her cheek. "They're going to love you."

Do you? she wanted to ask, but refrained. That wasn't a fair question, not until she was convinced of her own feelings for him.

Then again, perhaps she was sure and simply afraid he didn't love her in return. After one failed relationship, she was hesitant to venture out on that limb alone.

After they'd cleaned the kitchen, Cole threw on his shirt and helped Vi make the bed and tidy the room. He hadn't brought a change of clothes with him. She contemplated emptying a drawer for him and suggesting he bring clothes and toiletries with him.

Next week, she decided. Once their parents left.

Cole left the bedroom while Violet dressed, and when she emerged a few minutes later, she found him sitting at the kitchen table reading one of her silly gossip magazines.

She paused to study him as she'd done before. He looked so cute and quite at home. Closing her eyes, she tried to imagine him holding their baby. The picture came more easily than she might have anticipated.

Diamond Girl disrupted the peaceful scene when she sauntered in from the living room, meowing loudly. Stripes followed cautiously, as usual.

"What's up?" Cole asked the cat, setting down the magazine.

Diamond Girl brushed up against his leg. While Violet watched from her hidden post around the corner, he got up, located the kitty chow in the pantry and filled the empty bowl on the floor next to the fridge. Diamond Girl ate as if she was starving. Which she wasn't.

"Good cat." He scratched her head. Stripes refused to come out from under the table.

Violet fell a little harder for Cole. When she could speak without an emotional quiver in her voice, she entered the kitchen, not letting on that she'd seen him.

"You don't have to stick around," she said. "I'm sure you have things to do."

"Uh, yeah." He stood there, his gaze reflecting his appreciation.

She'd traded in her robe for a full-length sundress that was too nice for lounging around the house and too casual for wearing outside. Truthfully, she'd wanted to impress Cole without going overboard. She also liked the dress because it flattered her figure even with her thickening middle.

"You look nice," he said.

"Thanks." He'd seen her naked many times now, yet her cheeks heated at his praise.

Violet didn't often feel pretty, not in her line of work. Denny used to compliment her on her outfits when they went out, picking her up and swinging her around in circles. He'd never had the chance to see her waist thicken and her breasts swell.

After the second miscarriage, he'd stopped picking her up and swinging her around. After the third, he'd stopped touching her altogether.

In his defense, he'd stayed by her side without any talk

of leaving. When the marriage disintegrated, she was the one who'd faced reality for the both of them and moved out.

Cole smiled, his gaze still glued to her. "I suppose I should hit the road."

He didn't appear eager to leave. She wasn't eager for him to go, either.

"If you want to stay, we could ride together."

"I need to shower and change."

"Sure. Of course." How could she have forgotten?

"Come early. We'll walk up to the apartment together."

"Don't you want to visit with your mom first? It's been a while since you've seen her."

"No."

"Cole!"

"I'd rather wait for you."

I'd rather stay in Mustang Valley, be with you forever.

She heard his voice in her head. Or was it in her heart? Definitely not out loud, here in this kitchen.

"I don't want to interfere," she protested.

He moved closer, pinning her with his intense stare as only he could. "Interfere. Please. I'm begging."

She thought he might kiss her. Find a way to slip her out of the sundress she'd taken such care to put on. It would be easy to wrap her arms around his neck and mold her body to his, but reservations prevented her. As attentive as he'd been, as obvious as he'd made his interest in her, he hadn't said what she needed to hear.

Perhaps that was the reason she chose not to offer him an empty drawer.

She'd given in often, including that first night in the Poco Dinero Bar. Granted, it had felt right then and didn't exactly feel wrong now. Yet she sighed and stepped out of his reach.

"Josh is probably leaving now to pick your mom up at the airport, and my folks will be here soon."

"I could bring you home later."

"Let's see how it goes."

"Okay."

She could sense him shutting down in response to her subtle dismissal. So much for living the fantasy. The mood had definitely altered, and Violet was the one responsible.

"I'll meet you at the ranch house about twelve forty-five," she said, and brushed his hair from his face. She wasn't that ready to let go.

"Sounds good."

At the door, he kissed her goodbye, and she felt the hesitancy in his touch.

Watching through her living room window as he drove away, she wondered if she'd been wrong to abruptly apply the brakes.

Pressing a hand to her stomach, she thought *no*. She and Cole were walking a fine line. He knew her expectations; she'd been clear about them from the start. The decision to meet them or not was his.

She hoped he didn't disappoint her.

Chapter Twelve

With seven people present and thirty-odd packing boxes pushed into corners, Josh and Cara's small apartment was incredibly crowded. Along with the four usual occupants, Cole and his mother were there. And Vi, of course.

She was in the kitchen, helping Cara fix cold drinks for everyone and a bottle for baby Kimberly. Cole tried to keep his eyes off Vi and would succeed in averting his gaze, only to return it the next moment.

Must be the outfit. She'd mentioned choosing the sundress to hide her tummy, probably not realizing how much it flattered the view from behind.

She caught him staring on her return trip to the living room, a glass in each hand. He supposed it was bound to happen, and smiled guiltily. A cool nod was her only response.

Apparently he was still in the doghouse.

It had been his intention to smooth things over with Vi, but unfortunately, there hadn't been much chance to talk after she met him at the ranch—twelve forty-five on the dot, not a minute before. First, Raquel was there, hustling and bustling about in preparation for the dinner party. Either she didn't know what was in store for her with Cole's mother, or she did know and was using the overambitious dinner as a distraction.

Second—and this Cole didn't notice until they were just outside the apartment—Vi was extremely anxious at the prospect of meeting his mother. Not the best time to bring up their earlier awkward parting.

He would, however, find an opportunity later tonight. If she was still willing. She may have changed her mind, and it would be his fault. She'd been feeling vulnerable and needing him to reassure her. Instead, he'd choked.

What a loser. His grandfather would be ashamed of him. He'd holler at Cole and remind him that he'd been raised better. Hell, Cole was ashamed of himself.

He and Vi were having a baby. He cared about her. He thought—no, knew—she was the kind of woman he could love. Putting his child first was the right thing to do, which included marrying the mother.

Yet he held back, doubting himself and his abilities to be a good husband and father. He had a job with no salary, and if he stayed in Mustang Valley, his only other prospect was training ponies for pennies and mustangs for free.

Returning to California, assuming Vi would go with him, might be an option, but he refused to mooch off his mother and his grandparents. At least at Dos Estrellas he was pulling his weight and contributing his fair share. At his grandfather's, he'd be given a pity job, one he didn't really want, and which would likely send one of his grandfather's workers to the unemployment line.

Rodeo seemed to be the only viable option, but even that was limited. Eventually, Cole would be getting too old to compete at a level where he could make decent money. He was also sorely out of practice, not having stepped in the arena since last November.

His situation could and would change if Josh and Gabe bought out his share of the ranch. Except they were as broke as he was.

Every direction he turned, he was met with a brick wall. How could he ask Vi to marry him when he had no real prospects? She was better off without him.

Again Cole heard his grandfather ranting and raving, accusing him of making excuses. The old man was right.

"Cole, don't just stand there," his mother insisted. "Come sit with us. I haven't seen you in ages."

She motioned to the already crowded couch. With one grandchild on each side of her and Josh perched on the arm next to Kimberly, that left only a small space at the other end.

Cole resisted at first. His mom was setting the stage. She liked being the center of attention, which having her family surrounding her would accomplish. In her defense, it couldn't be easy having both her sons move to another state at the same time and Josh taking her grandchildren with him.

"Sure." Cole squeezed in beside Nathan.

"Uncle Cole, this is my gramma." He pointed at his grandmother.

"Yes. And she's also my mother."

"Your mother?" The boy took several seconds to assimilate the information, glancing back and forth between the two adults. "You have a mother?"

"I do. And she's your dad's mother, too."

The little boy slapped his cheeks with his hands, and his eyes nearly bugged out of his head.

Everyone laughed, Cole's mother most of all. He relaxed. Maybe today would go better than he and Josh had anticipated. Her grandchildren's antics seemed to be softening her up. Plan A in operation.

"Did you get checked into the inn?" Cole asked.

Josh, Cara and the kids had picked her up from the airport and brought her to the ranch.

"Yes." She pinched Kimberly's chin affectionately while answering. "Maybe you can take me back tonight. If you don't mind."

"I, um…" Cole shot Vi a look.

"Don't tell me you're busy," his mother complained. "I miss you."

Vi's pointed stare said, *Take her to the inn.*

"'Course I will."

"Oh, good." His mother smiled.

Cole tried not to feel resentful or believe that his mom had orchestrated the entire exchange simply to satisfy her whims. He did love her and wanted to spend time with her. She just wasn't the easiest person to get along with.

"Miranda," Cara intervened, "do you have any idea what you'd like to do tomorrow?"

She sat across from Cole in one of the two dining chairs that had been brought into the living room for extra seating. Vi sat nearer to Josh, and Cole tried to recall if she'd chosen that chair intentionally.

"I'd love a tour of the town," his mother answered. "I'm sure a lot has changed since I was last here. Maybe we could have lunch at the Cowboy Up Café. I noticed when we drove by that it's still open. Anything, really, as long as we take the children."

She gave each one a loving squeeze, stopping only when they giggled.

"Josh." Cara turned to him. "I have an idea. Maybe your mother would like to see the house we're renting. I'm sure the landlord won't mind. I can call him and ask if he'll meet us with the key."

"What do you think, Mom?" Josh asked.

"If that's want you want." She couldn't sound less enthused. "But what about the children?"

"They can come. They've been before."

"All right." She sighed, as if seeing the house would be a huge concession on her part.

Cara fidgeted, and Cole felt sorry for her. She and Vi, who also appeared uncomfortable, had a lot to contend with, being members of the Dempsey clan. He said nothing, certain if he spoke his mind, his mother would retaliate.

"We could visit the mustang sanctuary," Cara said.

"Good idea." Cole thought the suggestion an excellent one. As a fellow horsewoman, his mother would appreciate all that Cara had done.

Or perhaps not.

"Maybe." Again, Miranda's tone reflected disinterest.

A thought struck Cole, one he hadn't considered before. Was his mother nervous about the upcoming dinner party with Raquel and Gabe? Could that account for her negativity? The more Cole thought about it, the more convinced he became that he was right.

"You must be looking forward to moving." Cole's mother surveyed the small apartment, her pinched features conveying her disdain.

"I am." Cara placed a hand to her chest. "Though I love this place."

"You lived here before Josh moved in, didn't you?"

"Yes. With my son."

"I'm truly sorry." For the first time since she arrived, Miranda expressed kindness to someone other than her grandchildren.

"It was hard to lose him, and I'll always miss him."

"No one ever recovers completely from the death of a child."

"You're right." Cara smiled warmly at Nathan and Kimberly. "I'm grateful for these two. They've helped fill the holes in my heart."

It was sweet of her to say—and completely the wrong thing. Cole's mother instantly stiffened. Did she think she was being pushed aside in her grandchildren's lives in order to make room for Cara?

Cole wanted to stand up and shout, "You're wrong!" Again he refrained, but it was getting harder.

"I really don't know why you two are renting a house," his mother said, "when you could move back to California. Wouldn't that make more sense?"

"I can't leave the ranch." Josh pushed himself up from the couch arm and raked his fingers through his hair, something he tended to do when he was angry or frustrated.

Cole wished he could exercise the same kind of restraint. He tended to vent by causing trouble or taking unnecessary risks, a lot of those on the back of a bull or bucking bronc.

"Why not?" his mother demanded. "You hated the ranch, as I recall."

"Not anymore," Josh said.

"Well, that's an about-face."

"There's also the mustang sanctuary. Cara has invested a lot of time and effort into it. She has a brand-new equine therapy program that's growing weekly and making a real name for itself. She can't bail now. There's no one else to run it."

"I suppose."

Both children had started to get restless. They were in good company, Cole thought.

Nathan climbed down from the couch and went straight to Josh, pulling on his shirt. "I hungry, Daddy."

Josh patted his head. "We're eating soon."

Not soon enough. Cole hoped they all survived until the dinner.

"There are wild mustangs in California, too," his mother said. "You could move the sanctuary there."

Would she ever give it a rest?

"We're not moving," Josh said. "Besides, I happen to enjoy ranching, and as it turns out, I'm pretty good at it."

"Like your father."

Josh laughed. "I'll take that as a compliment."

"Hmm."

Cole wouldn't have thought it possible, but his mother actually turned up her nose.

What would she say if she knew Josh and Gabe wanted to buy out Cole's share? He hadn't told her yet, feeling it was Josh's place. Now, he was glad he'd kept his mouth shut.

His mother deftly changed the subject. "Violet, tell me. Are you also from the area?"

"No. I grew up in Seattle. Found my way here ten years ago by accident and stayed."

Cole gave Vi credit; she was handling his mom like a pro.

"Pregnancy suits you. You're very pretty."

Vi blushed at his mother's complement, and Cole wished he was sitting next to her.

"I have another ultrasound scheduled in two weeks. I'm hoping the doctor will be able to tell us the sex of the baby, though it's a little early."

Cole blinked. He wasn't sure which took him further aback—that Vi had an ultrasound scheduled she hadn't told him about or her use of the word *us*.

"Son, if you don't mind me asking…" His mother leaned forward. "How are you going to support the baby? From what Josh says, you two aren't drawing salaries from the ranch."

Had she really just asked that?

Vi also waited for him to answer. Cole ground his teeth together. He didn't need to be grilled in front of an audience.

"Mom." Josh's warning was unmistakable.

"It's a reasonable question," she protested.

"And none of your business."

She ignored Josh. "You should come home to California, Cole. You have a job waiting for you there."

Now she was manipulating *him*, having failed with Josh. Cole wanted to be angry. He *was* angry, but at himself more than his mother, as she was echoing his own sentiments and doubts.

"I'm not moving, either," he said.

"Bring Violet and the baby with you."

"Ma'am," Vi interrupted. "I can't leave—"

Cole's mother cut her off before she could say more. "I told you to call me Miranda."

"Miranda." Vi drew in a breath. "Mustang Valley is my home."

"Please say you'll think about it. I can't bear not having any of my grandchildren near me."

Josh went to Cara and placed his hands on the back of her chair. "It's almost two. Raquel will be ringing the dinner bell any minute."

Cara stood and said brightly, "I don't know about the rest of you, but I'm getting hungry."

A party. In the house where Cole's mother once lived. Where his father's long-time companion now resided with her grown son. Cole gave it ten minutes at most before all hell broke loose.

As they walked down the stairs, she held Nathan's hand. "Josh, who watches the children while you work?"

Cara hurriedly jumped in with an answer. "I do, a lot of the time."

"What about when you're at the sanctuary?"

"We have a babysitter," Josh said, not admitting it was Raquel who watched the kids most days.

One by one, they reached the ground floor. The short walk to the house passed pleasantly enough. Then, right on schedule, just as they entered the house through the kitchen door, the moment Cole had been dreading came.

Nathan ran ahead of everyone and straight for Raquel, calling, *"Abuela!"*

Cole's mother's lips thinned to a flat line and her eyes burned with fury. She spoke enough Spanish to recognize the word for *grandmother*.

COLE CORNERED VIOLET in the hallway outside the kitchen as she returned from the restroom. Everyone else was in the living room, except for Raquel and Cara. Violet had been helping them set up the dining room when she suddenly needed to excuse herself, an occurrence happening more and more frequently of late.

"You've been avoiding me," he said.

"Not at all. Raquel needed a hand."

He was right, of course. Vi had been avoiding him.

"I'm sorry about my mom."

She shrugged. It wasn't Cole's fault the visit in the apartment had been awful. But while Miranda's behavior was inexcusable, she'd asked some important questions. Ones Violet also wanted answered.

He moved closer. "At least she's behaving so far."

"Thank goodness." Violet strived to keep her voice light. In actuality, her emotions were running high. It had been that kind of day.

Miranda had practically unraveled when Nathan called Raquel *abuela*. Apparently, however, she'd refused to give Raquel the satisfaction of a response, and had quickly collected herself. The remnants of her fury were still present, though, in the cool way she treated the other woman.

Violet's parents were also in a snit. They'd arrived a short while ago, her mother agitated and her father grim-faced. They did manage to put on a good front with the rest of the guests—especially Cara's parents, who were lovely—while bickering and exchanging digs when they thought no one was looking or listening.

The only really happy people in the room were Raquel and Reese's father, Theo, who both seemed unaware of the tension simmering beneath the surface.

"Your mom hasn't stopped talking about the baby," Cole said to Violet.

"Do you mind?" Now that she'd officially passed the twelve-week mark, she felt ready to talk with people.

"Are you kidding?" Cole grinned. "Bring it on."

"Really?"

"I may not have this all figured out yet, but that doesn't mean I'm not excited."

She'd trust his answer more if not for the glaring lack of a twinkle in his eyes.

"Is your mom always so direct?"

"Always. Especially when she's on a mission." His grin faded. "Don't say I didn't warn you."

"I can understand. She's probably lonely."

"Enough about my mother." He lowered his head until his mouth was level with Violet's ear. Before today, she'd have turned to him for a kiss. But not here and not now. "Are we still on for later? This shindig should be over by four."

She was the one who'd wanted to have a conversation with him. Still, she hesitated. "You promised to drive your mom to the inn."

"That'll take a half hour tops."

"She wants to visit with you and mine wants to take me shopping."

"Maternity clothes?" His glance traveled to her middle.

Violet couldn't help herself and laughed. It felt good after the past exhausting ninety minutes. "Shoe shopping. For her. As if she needs more shoes." Violet sobered. "It's really an excuse. I'm sure she wants to talk about Dad and the divorce. She's convinced he's trying to deprive her of her rightful share. I'm pretty sure she's buying up everything in sight before the accountants finish with the audit."

"Audit? Of what?"

"Their marital assets." Violet raised a hand. "Please don't ask me. The whole thing just boggles my mind."

"I'm sorry, sweetie."

He hadn't used any terms of endearment since the day they'd rushed to the hospital. Then, he'd been trying to calm her fears.

Today, however, he said the word softly, with affection. She discovered she longed to hear it again in a far more private setting.

"Hey, you two, hurry up." Raquel poked her head around the corner. "We're ready to eat."

"Here goes nothing," Cole said.

Violet met his intimate gaze. All at once, her reservations and her irritation melted away. He was once again the man she'd fallen for.

Because there were too many of them to sit at the dining room table, Raquel had opted for a serve-and-seat-yourself buffet. She'd spared nothing, and the spread of food was fit for a king.

The only exception was the children. They sat at a child-size table Josh had purchased secondhand a few weeks ago. Normally, it was kept in the kitchen. Today Raquel had relocated it to the dining room.

Violet had always wanted a table and chairs like that for her own children.

Children? She hadn't yet had this baby, and she was already thinking ahead to another one. With Cole? She studied him from a distance—and was promptly cut short when Reese accosted her.

"I'm so excited for you." Reese grabbed her and hugged her. "I just had to tell you again."

"She's good at keeping a secret." Cara came over to join them, leveling a finger at Violet. "That's for sure." She'd known about the baby only because Josh had spilled the beans.

The men were less demonstrative, but enthusiastic nonetheless with their well-wishing. Reese's father especially.

"Not that we're related," Theo said to Cole and Violet, "but I feel like I'm going to be a grandfather."

"And me a grandmother," Raquel added enthusiastically.

Everyone went still, and Miranda sucked in a sharp breath.

Uh-oh. So much for Violet basking in the attention. The atmosphere in the room instantly changed. Even plates laden with the delicious fare didn't make a difference.

Cole stayed steadfastly at Violet's side as if he could shield her from all the negativity. They found two seats on the living room sofa and dug in.

"This is delicious." Violet's mother turned to Raquel. "You've always been such a good cook."

"Gracias." Raquel beamed. Was she truly immune to the tension or just choosing to pretend all was well?

Violet's parents sat at opposite ends of the room. Perhaps things between them were worse than she had initially thought. Her mother kept up a lively conversation with anyone who would listen, except for her husband, whom she ignored. Violet recognized the often used ploy.

"Reese and Gabe tell me the ranch is doing better," Theo commented around a bite of beef enchilada. "That this last quarter has seen a decrease in losses."

"Dad!" Reese sighed wearily. "What did I tell you?"

"That's right." He looked apologetic from where he sat in the leather chair that had once been August's favorite. "I was warned I'm not allowed to talk business at dinner."

"I agree with your daughter," Raquel replied good-naturedly. "But in all these years, I haven't been able to stop them. It's part of ranching." Her glance encompassed not only Gabe but also Cole and Josh, as if they, too, were her sons.

Miranda visibly stiffened, her fork clutched tightly in her hand. Cole tensed, probably bracing himself should his mother choose to lash out. After a moment with no outburst, he marginally relaxed.

"It's okay," Gabe told Theo. "You can talk business. I'm actually happy to report that things are improving. Turns out we may not have to wait until the fall sale. There's a buyer from Oklahoma coming out next week to look at our steers. If he likes what he sees, he's prepared to make an offer."

"I know the one you're talking about," Theo said. "He wouldn't be making the trip if he wasn't serious."

Violet couldn't help noting no one mentioned the mustang sanctuary and equine therapy program, though both played a large role in the ranch's financial recovery. The rent Cara paid for her share of the pastureland and her recent contribution to the delinquent property taxes had made a significant difference to the decrease in losses.

"There's still a lot of work ahead," Josh cautioned. "We aren't yet operating in the black."

"How soon until you are?" Miranda asked. "Operating in the black?" She'd barely touched her food after Raquel's earlier comment, not that she'd been wolfing her meal down to begin with.

"No one's sure," Josh said. "We agreed to assess things at the end of a year, then move forward carefully and conservatively."

"This November then?"

"More like December."

Violet understood Josh's reluctance. There was always the chance of a snafu. The buyer from Oklahoma might change his mind or a check from the fall sale bounce.

"But we're optimistic," Josh said.

"I'm glad to hear that." Miranda set her plate down on the coffee table.

Initially, Violet thought it was because the children had finished eating and came charging into the living room, fighting each other for a place on Josh's lap. She was wrong. Miranda was on a mission, exactly as Cole had predicted.

"With the state of the ranch improving, there's no reason for both you and Cole to remain here. Certainly one of you can come home."

Violet heard Cole groan under his breath. Without thinking, she reached over and laid a hand on his arm.

"California?" Violet's mother gasped softly. "Darling, you're not moving, are you?"

"No, Mom."

"No one's moving," Cole reiterated through clenched teeth.

"Why not?" Miranda asked. "You have a job and a home in California. You'll need both with a baby on the way."

"The boys can't leave." Theo chuckled amiably. "Someone needs to be in charge, now that Gabe's agreed to manage the Small Change for me full-time. Dos Estrellas can't operate on its own."

All eyes flew to Gabe. Violet admitted to being shocked by the news, though anyone should have seen it coming. Gabe had been dividing his time between the neighboring ranches for months.

"It only makes sense." Gabe took Reese's hand and fingered her sparkling engagement ring. "We are getting married."

"I'll be leaving the place to Reese one of these days," Theo continued, his face alive with joy. "And any grandchildren they give me, which I hope are many."

"Daddy," Reese exclaimed. "Don't talk like that. You're not going anywhere."

"My intentions, exactly. I'm just saying, Dos Estrellas shouldn't take any steps back after taking so many forward. Good as Gabe is, expecting him to manage both ranches is asking too much."

Miranda sat stoically in her chair.

"Congratulations." Cara sent Gabe a fond smile. She was the only one in the room thinking of him.

The children, perhaps in response to the mixed moods of the adults, began whining and complaining.

"I bet they could use a nap." Raquel started to rise.

Cara beat her to the punch. "I'll take them to the apartment. You all keep visiting."

Violet silently commended her friend. Raquel assuming charge of the children would no doubt push Miranda over the edge.

Once Cara and the children were gone, conversation started again, though haltingly. As one by one people finished their dinner, Violet gathered their plates. She returned from her second trip to the kitchen and sat, listening to her mother's conversation with Raquel.

"You have such a beautiful home. I love the antiques. And that oil painting is absolutely gorgeous."

"August took a lot of pride in this place."

Violet felt her stomach tighten. Observing Cole, she saw the storm clouds gathering on his face.

Her mother turned to Miranda. "If I may ask, how come you didn't get the house in the divorce? Doesn't it usually go to the wife? Especially when she has children."

The silence that followed was louder than any cannon fire.

"Mom!" Violet exclaimed, finding her voice.

Miranda appeared to fold in on herself. She glared openly at Raquel, no longer trying to hide her dislike. Raquel's mouth hung open in surprise and confusion.

"What?" Violet's mother asked innocently, looking around the room. "I'm curious."

And intent on embarrassing her husband. Already, his face had turned a vivid scarlet.

"That's enough, Julia," he said sharply.

"You always make such a big deal out of things. Everyone divorces these days. It's not a taboo subject."

Before Violet's father could muster a response, Miranda said, "I left because of *her*. After she stole my husband."

Raquel shifted nervously.

"That's enough, Mom." Cole spoke brusquely.

"She asked, I answered."

As if that was an excuse.

"How could you?" Violet demanded of her mother.

"You're overreacting, darling."

Violet decided she hadn't reacted enough, and not only about this.

Miranda squared her shoulders. "I want my sons to come home. I don't see anything wrong with that."

"For the tenth time," Josh said, "I'm not leaving Mustang Valley."

"Josh, please—"

"In fact, Cara and I are getting married. We were waiting to make an announcement."

"No!"

"Thanks for your support," Josh said snidely.

Tears blurred Violet's vision. She couldn't believe her parents would snipe at each other and that Cole's mother would be so blatantly rude. They should all be ashamed of themselves.

A painful sob lodged in her throat, making breathing difficult, and she began to shake. All at once a hand gripped her arm, firm and insistent. It belonged to Cole.

"Come on." He pulled her up from the sofa. "Let's get out of here."

She shook her head. How could she leave? This train wreck wasn't over.

"Think of the baby."

Yes. He was right. Dr. Medina had warned her against stress.

Blindly following Cole, Violet let him lead her from the room, vaguely aware of her mother and Miranda calling their names.

Chapter Thirteen

Cole didn't ask where Violet wanted to go and she didn't object when he steered his truck in the direction of her house. Three minutes into the drive, her cell phone rang.

Recognizing the ring tone, she answered without saying hello. "Now's not a good time, Mom."

"Your dad and I are sorry."

"Okay."

"That's it?"

"I'm hardly the only one you should be apologizing to."

Cole looked over at her often as she talked. She held herself together, but just barely.

"Yes, well." Her mother hated admitting she was wrong or had made a mistake. "We'll be there shortly. We can talk."

Violet didn't hesitate. "No, go back to the resort."

"Later then?"

"Not later, either."

"You're annoyed."

"Yes, Mom, I'm annoyed. What do you think? You were completely out of line and ungracious. Raquel has always been kind to you. I thought you two were friends."

"Violet, please. What about our shopping trip?"

"I'll call you in the morning. Goodbye, Mom."

She didn't talk the rest of the drive, which lasted only a few more minutes.

"Sweetie—"

"Not now, Cole." She cut him off, too, then blew out a woeful sigh. "Sorry. I shouldn't snap at you. It's just that what happened back there was a terrible disaster. Humiliating. I don't ever want to be like them."

"Tell me about it. My mom is a piece of work."

"No more than my mom."

At Violet's house, Cole pulled up to the curb and captured her hand. "We'll get through this."

"Right." She took comfort from his touch. He more than anyone understood having difficult parents.

"Come on. Let's get you off your feet."

Inside, she went directly to her bedroom and donned shorts and a T-shirt, wishing she could shed the events of the past few hours as easily as she did her sundress. Cole was waiting for her in the kitchen. He'd kept himself busy by feeding the cats. Her mood lifted a tiny bit.

Should she invite him to spend the night again? Did he expect it?

Grabbing a diet soda from the fridge, she sat at the table.

"I thought you were avoiding caffeine."

"I need a boost." She took a long draw on the soda. "One tiny fall off the wagon won't hurt."

"What are you going to do about your folks?"

"I don't know yet. Their divorce is getting out of control, and they're hurting so many people. Talk to them again, I guess."

"I can't believe Josh and Cara are getting married."

"Why?" She stared at Cole in astonishment. "They're in love."

He reclined in his chair and stretched out his legs. "Josh has been down that road before. It didn't go well."

"Cara's no addict. She hasn't been in and out of rehab."

"Of course not. I'm just saying he's been married before and it tanked. I think he'd be a little leery about jumping in again, considering he's only been divorced nine months."

"One bad marriage doesn't mean a second one will fail."

"I suppose."

"Is it just Josh and Cara or are you anti-marriage in general?"

She hadn't considered that possibility before, but in a way it made sense and would explain his reluctance.

"I don't know. I've seen a lot of broken marriages. My parents divorced when I was young. Yours are in the process and can barely stay in the same room without tearing into each other. Cara's marriage hit the skids after just five years. Yours, too."

"It's not that simple. I had three miscarriages and Cara's son died. Josh's wife got addicted to pain pills after her car crash. I can tell you from personal experience, losses are damn hard on a relationship. You think they'll bring two people closer together, only the exact opposite is true. It rips them apart."

"My parents didn't have a loss. Or yours."

"Wow, Cole. You're kind of harsh." She had a difficult time believing what she was hearing. "The death of love isn't any less of a loss."

"You're right." He sat up and pulled in his legs. "I guess I don't have a good opinion of marriage. I watched my parents hurt not only one another but Josh and me, too."

"Is that why you haven't asked me to marry you?"

"I have."

"You've hinted. Not the same thing."

"You were the one who insisted we wait." His tone had acquired an edge.

"In the beginning, yes, I did. I wanted for us to make progress first."

"We've been together pretty much every day since I learned about the baby. I'd say we're making great progress."

She told herself they were mad at their parents and unintentionally taking it out on each other. But the resemblance to her parents' bickering bothered her.

"We're still getting acquainted," she said. "Building on our initial connection. A little late, I suppose."

"Most people build on their connection before getting married."

She took a moment to mentally regroup, not quite sure how they'd gone from discussing their parents to his lack of a proposal.

"I get that you're gun-shy," she conceded.

"Aren't you?"

"Some." She stared at him pointedly. "But I'm willing to make a commitment."

"Wait a minute." He frowned. "I have committed. I'm staying in Mustang Valley. Not returning to the rodeo circuit."

"Temporarily."

He didn't address her comment. "I'm trying, Vi. I'm not moving back to California. I didn't leave your side when we were at the hospital, and I stayed with you for three days when you needed help. I did all those things for only one reason."

"The baby." She finished for him.

"You and the baby. But you're the one I care about the most. I fully expect to love our kid when he or she is born. Until then, you're my first priority."

First priority. Not exactly a romantic declaration, which, Violet realized, was what she wanted. What she deserved.

"I'm not saying marriage is off the table," he continued.

Her brows shot up. "From what I can tell, it was never on the table."

He spoke slowly and with a pronounced lack of conviction. "I think we should live together first."

She gave a dry laugh. "I see. We maintain an escape plan until we're sure."

"Not what I said."

He'd implied it. "I don't need a husband. I can raise this baby alone."

"Now you're being obstinate."

Her eyes filled with tears and her throat burned. Dammit, she refused to be emotional. It was imperative she remain in control.

Cole must have sensed her fragile state and asked, "Why don't we finish this discussion later? We've both had a rough afternoon."

"That's our problem, Cole. We've postponed when we should have been talking."

"I don't disagree. But I still say this isn't the best day. We're upset. We watched our parents put on a ridiculous show. Let's wait for yours to go home tomorrow. Hopefully, they won't delay their departure again."

"You're stalling." Anger bloomed inside Violet. She felt its heat and power.

"What I'm suggesting is reasonable, Vi. We have time."

"Be honest. You don't want this baby."

"A part of me does. Very much. Another part of me worries that I'll be a terrible father, like my own."

"Then it's me you don't want."

"You're angry and you're not listening to me."

She hated that he was right, and willed her pounding heart rate to slow.

"I'm overwhelmed." He paused, seeming to search for

the right words to express himself without hurting her. "My life is quickly moving in a direction I hadn't anticipated, and I can't keep up."

"Mine, too."

"I've lost the one job I ever had. Rodeoing. Given up the only home I really remember. My grandparents' place in California. And I'm about to become a father when I wasn't planning on it for several more years. Yeah, I get it," he stated before she could speak. "You weren't planning on a baby, either. But it's been your dream. You're thrilled even though the circumstances aren't ideal."

Right again.

She wiped at her damp cheeks. "I don't casually sleep with men."

"Of course not. I never thought that for one second."

"I only did with you because you're important to me. I liked you. A lot. I have from the time you came to Dos Estrellas, though I didn't always show it."

She hoped he saw she was putting herself out there.

He must have for his voice softened. "We've rushed our relationship. Most people start out dating, then they fall in love, get married and have kids. We're doing things backward."

She nodded contemplatively and traveled further out on the limb. "I might be a little in love with you."

The long pause that followed was smothering. Her chest ached from oxygen deprivation. When he finally spoke, she barely heard him over the din in her ears.

"You know I haven't had any lasting relationships except for the one, and she lied to me."

The pregnant woman who'd claimed Cole was the father of her baby in order to snare him.

Violet stared at him incredulously. "Do you think I'm trying to trap you?"

"No." He scowled as if to emphasize his denial.

"Because I meant what I said. I don't need you to raise this baby."

"I'm simply asking for more time. It's only been a month."

"You've spent the night here. We've slept together. You said things to me. Things I believed."

"I wasn't lying."

The world she'd envisioned for herself felt as if it was breaking into small pieces and slipping between her fingers. "It's stupid, I know, but I thought you'd change."

"I have changed," he said. "Just, apparently, not into the man you want."

She'd hurt him. It was evident by his pained features.

"It's not that I can't or won't be that man, but you have to be more patient with me."

"I'm trying, Cole. You don't make it easy. You send mixed signals. When we're intimate, you make me believe what we have is real and full of potential. Then you pull away. Withdraw. Like you are now."

"You do, too. Send mixed signals."

Did she?

"One minute you're pressuring me to commit. The next, you're claiming you don't need me."

She stood, propelled by anger and disappointment. "You're right. We've been rushing this. Maybe we should take a break. Retreat to our separate corners for a while."

"I see," he said coolly.

"What do you have to be mad about? I'm giving you what you want. Space. Freedom. No strings."

"You don't like the way the conversation's going, so you suddenly decide we're through and I should go home."

She rubbed her temple. "I have a headache."

He stood abruptly. "However this turns out, I promise to take care of you and the baby."

"Sounds…final."

"I only asked for time. You're the one suggesting we split."

"A break isn't splitting. You're making me out to be the bad guy."

"I'm not like my brothers, Vi. I think that's what you're hoping for. A man who's ready to settle down and start a family. Unfortunately, you're stuck with me."

She opened her mouth to speak, only to snap it shut. He would take what she said wrong or twist her words. Their conversation had degraded to that extent.

"I really think you should go."

"This isn't what I want, Vi."

Her temper flared. She knew she should bite her tongue, but she didn't. "The problem is you don't know what you want. Or you do and it isn't me."

"Not true."

"No, no. You don't want *pregnant* me."

He shook his head. "I guess I just got my walking papers."

She didn't correct him.

"I'll call you tomorrow," he said.

"I'll call *you*. When I feel like talking."

She didn't follow him to the entryway. Rather, she stood there in the kitchen, listening to the sound of his retreating footsteps and, seconds later, the closing door.

Violet slumped into the chair, all the strength in her legs having seeped away, and burst into tears. She'd just sent the father of her child away, possibly for good.

It might be for best, only it felt more like the biggest mistake of her life.

As much as she'd hoped differently, they simply weren't

in the same place at the same time. And while she couldn't fault Cole entirely, she did. For now.

Maybe later, she'd look at this more objectively. Maybe later, she'd admit the truth. To herself, at least. She didn't really want to raise her child alone.

THE CATTLE BUYER from Oklahoma was due in less than a half hour. Joey had been assigned the task of waiting for the man's arrival at the ranch and then driving him out to meet Cole, Josh and Gabe in section four, where most of the young steers were currently pastured.

Normally, Vi would have been the one to drive the buyer. Instead, she'd headed home at lunchtime, still adhering to her part-time schedule. Cole thought she might also be avoiding him. They'd been doing that a lot this past week, avoiding each other. Conversing only when necessary. Glancing away when the other approached. Coming up with tasks needing immediate attention as an excuse to leave.

He was growing tired of it, and of the crummy way he felt.

Crummy? Who was he kidding? The *guilty* way he felt.

He especially hated the emotionally damaged expression Vi continually wore. She was better off without him. Perhaps they'd been foolish to think they could make a go of it. He may have been what she wanted that night in the bar—a diversion to help her forget the news of her parents' divorce—but he wasn't what she needed for the long haul. Cole had proved that by failing to rise so much as an inch above the very low relationship bar he'd set for himself.

The problem was, he missed her like crazy. He could easily, and often did, conjure up her smile, with its gorgeous, sexy dimples. And those green eyes of hers. One minute they'd be flashing with delight, warmth or humor.

The next, they'd spark with anger or indignation. Regardless of her mood, she captivated him.

Not that he liked it when she was mad at him. He did, however, enjoy the many facets of her moods, if only to watch her expressions change as if a magic wand had been waved across her face.

Her passion for life, her job and her unborn child both inspired and enthralled him. When that passion was directed at Cole, it elevated him to the best version of himself. Though, apparently, he didn't stay there long and came crashing right back down to ground level. Take last week, for example.

He hadn't wanted things to end between them—it was never his intent. Truthfully, he wasn't completely sure they *had* ended things until yesterday, when Vi turned abruptly and made a beeline for the tack room rather than cross paths with him.

Her message couldn't have been any louder or clearer and it had hit him like a fastball to the chest. The pain had been immediate and left a huge hollow space inside him where his heart had once resided.

The encounter also caused him to realize how much he'd hurt her. Perhaps irreparably. He hadn't wanted that, either, but Cole seemed destined for circumstances that changed swiftly and often, neither to his liking nor under his control.

Well, that last part might be a stretch. He could have done one or two things differently.

"Hey, Cole," Josh called. "Get your head in the game, will you? This meeting is important. What's wrong with you, anyway?"

"Nothing."

Cole shook himself, both physically and mentally, but it didn't clear the heavy fog of despair surrounding him.

They'd ridden out to section four in Josh's truck. Cole had volunteered to drive, but apparently, after the fiasco when he'd bottomed out in the ravine, he wasn't considered trustworthy.

"If you ask me, he's feeling sorry for himself." Gabe sent a heated glare in his direction. "I would if I were in his shoes."

"Funny." Cole said drily.

"You blew it, brother."

He hadn't told anyone about his disagreement with Vi. He wasn't sure she had, either. Like him, she kept quiet about her personal problems, revealing only bits and pieces. His family, however, was perceptive and accomplished at deciphering bits and pieces.

Cole had been deflecting jabs for the past couple days, mostly from Josh and Gabe, through Raquel had gotten in on the action. Vi, from what he'd seen and heard, was receiving only support and sympathy.

No one in the family was happy about their fight. They acted as if Cole had argued with them rather than Vi.

The one bright note was that all the parents had gone home. Before leaving, Julia and Edgar Hathaway apologized to Raquel for the scene they'd caused. Cole's mother had not. Not to him and Josh and not to Cara, her future daughter-in-law. Cole doubted she'd be returning to Mustang Valley any time soon and continued to press her case for one of them to move home.

"Lay off me, will you?" Cole complained. Leaning his back on the truck door, he tugged his hat low to shade his face and block his view of his brothers.

Not to be ignored, Gabe came up beside him and propped an elbow on the hood. "You brought this on yourself," he said, without a trace of sympathy.

Not entirely by himself. Disagreements required two or

more people. But Gabe and the other Dempseys had known Vi for over ten years and loved her like family. Their relationship with Cole was new and untried. Put in a position to choose sides, they'd likely pick Vi's.

Today, that left the three brothers standing awkwardly in the middle of Dos Estrellas's six hundred acres as they waited for the cattle buyer who could, if he liked the steers, solve most of their financial problems.

"You should marry her," Gabe said.

"You think I didn't ask?"

Josh sauntered over. "Did you?"

"What? You two get together ahead of time and strategize?" Cole glanced accusingly at Gabe first, then Josh.

"Answer the question."

"Not exactly." Cole would have tugged his hat lower on his face if he thought it would do any good.

Instead, he glanced at his phone, checking the time, then studied the horizon and the dirt road leading to the pasture gate. "Shouldn't Joey and this Maitlin guy be here? It's after two."

"Why not?" Gabe move closer. "She not good enough for you? She's having your baby."

"She's too good for me." Cole chuckled bitterly. "I promised her I'd take care of her and the baby. Except I can't. Not without some kind of salary coming in. The only way I know of to earn money is rodeoing. Only she doesn't want me to go on the road. What the hell else do I have to offer her? Third ownership in a ranch that isn't turning a profit?"

Josh shook his head dismally. "You're right. She is too good for you."

"You have an answer? Because I'm all ears."

Gabe didn't say anything, but there was a noticeable change in his expression as the hard set of his jaw lessened.

Thankfully, Cole was spared further interrogation by the appearance of a vehicle in the distance, rumbling along the dirt road that cut across the adjoining section. "Looks like our buyer is here."

Cole was less sure of the sale going through than his brothers, who both assumed all that remained was to sign on the dotted line. Perhaps he'd been disappointed once too often and didn't like counting on something before it was a done deal.

He did understand their excitement even if he couldn't share it. With over four hundred steers to sell, and current prices on the rise, they could make a fair profit.

More than that, the ranch would have a surplus of cash, something they'd done without since Cole's father became sick. They hadn't discussed in detail what they'd do with the money if the sale went through, what bills they'd pay after the balance owed to the cancer treatment center.

When the truck with Joey and Maitlin arrived, they made introductions all around and proceeded to the fence line for a gander at the steers. The long-distance inspection was followed by a closer one. Joey stayed behind while the four men traveled in one truck, driving down a ridge that took them nearer to the herd. They stopped when the steers appeared uneasy, not wanting them to run, and got out, approaching the rest of the way on foot.

The inspection took more than an hour. Maitlin had a lot of questions. He recorded voice notes on his phone and took a dozen pictures. Afterward came the negotiations. Cole let Gabe take the lead, as the most knowledgeable, with Josh, as ranch manager, making contributions. Cole mostly observed. And learned.

Would it matter? If he left Mustang Valley, he'd never put his newfound learning to use.

What with all the notes and pictures Maitlin took, Cole

expected the cattle buyer to thank them for their trouble, leave and, hopefully, call later with a lowball offer. Instead, he made one right then and there.

Gabe countered as smoothly as if he'd been expecting it all along. Maitlin smiled, and the negotiations were under way. In the end, they reached a deal and shook hands to seal it. Maitlin pulled a checkbook from his pocket and wrote one out to cover the down payment. The transport trucks would arrive within the next two to three days and the remaining funds sent by wire for deposit into the ranch checking account.

Cole was admittedly impressed by his brother. The deal wasn't a bad one. They'd talked ahead of time, deciding on the minimum price they'd take. Gabe had negotiated an amount that was marginally better.

Maitlin declined their invitation to dinner. He was due in St. Johns by seven the next morning.

"Good job," Cole said, when Maitlin drove off with Joey.

"Damn good." Josh clapped Gabe hard on the shoulder. "Shall we celebrate? Meet up at the Poco Dinero after dinner?"

The bar where Cole and Vi's relationship began. Hard to believe nearly three and a half months had passed since then. Hard to believe their relationship had ended before it really began.

"I'll check with Reese," Gabe said. "What about Cara?"

Josh grinned. "I'm sure she'll be up for it." He turned to Cole. "Guess there's no point in you asking Violet."

"She might come if the whole family's going. She's more likely to come if I stay away."

"Dammit, Cole." Gabe blew out an exasperated breath. "You screwed up."

He felt compelled to defend himself. "Did it ever occur to you, to either of you, that she screwed up?"

Josh scowled. "You can't be serious."

"It's complicated."

"Only if you let it be. What you need to do is go to her, tell her you're sorry, get down on your knees and beg her forgiveness. Promise whatever you have to promise. I did that with Cara."

"I can't."

"You're an idiot."

"I'm as good as broke. How can I go to her when I have nothing?"

"Take this." Gabe folded the down payment check in half and slipped it into Cole's shirt pocket. "That ought to be enough."

Cole whipped the check out and pushed it at Gabe. "No way."

"Consider it the first payment for your share of the ranch." Gabe looked to Josh for confirmation. "We'll pay you more when the wire comes in for the balance."

Josh nodded his approval.

"No." Cole laughed. "Are you nuts? There are bills to pay. The ranch needs this money." Again he tried to return the check to Gabe.

"You want out, Cole. You have from day one." Gabe gave him a hard stare. "Here's your chance. You'll have more than enough money to take care of your child. Then you can return to the rodeo circuit or go to California. Whatever you want."

Cole fingered the check. He thought of his last bull ride, of the excitement coursing through him and the thrill of competing in the finals.

It paled in comparison to holding Vi in his arms and seeing the image of their child on the ultrasound screen.

"Do you think it's possible? To be happily married? To love someone for the rest of your life?"

"Damn straight I do." Gabe grinned. "I'm counting on it."

"Kind of a strange remark, coming from a guy whose parents never married."

"It worked for them. It wouldn't work for Reese and me. A commitment is important to her. Marriage. The whole nine yards. I wouldn't ask her to settle for less."

"Ditto for Cara," Josh said.

Cole had asked Vi to settle. He'd suggested they live together. Had that been because, deep down, he was afraid of taking that final step? One that might land him in the same position as his parents?

"Take a few days and think about it," Josh said.

Cole wasn't sure his brother was advising him to think about marrying Vi or taking the check and leaving.

"What about your wedding?" he asked Gabe. "I don't want to miss it."

"You can fly back."

He wished Gabe had made more of an objection.

Unfolding the check, Cole stared at it. The amount was no pittance. This was what he'd wanted the day the attorney read his father's will. A fistful of money. Now, he had it.

What he didn't have, something he'd vowed to earn and keep, was the respect of his brothers. That was the reason he'd sold his roping horses last fall.

Could he leave without it? Was having enough money to support his child worth the trade-off?

Believing he had the answer, he pocketed the check, walked around to the passenger side door and climbed into the truck.

Chapter Fourteen

Violet sat at the desk in the shed, staring at the work schedule for the next two weeks. She could have switched on the small lamp beside her. Today, she preferred the sunlight filtering in through the window, grimy panes, cobwebs and all, to an artificial yellow glow.

All at once, the names and dates on the schedule floated before her eyes as a wave of intense nausea hit.

"No," she mumbled, "not again."

Stacking her arms on the desk, she laid her head down and waited for the queasiness to pass. It wasn't entirely unusual for morning sickness to continue into the second trimester. She'd been feeling a lot better these past few weeks, then, bam! She was back to this uneasy roller-coaster ride.

She kept assuring herself the lousy way she felt was entirely the result of changes in her body due to pregnancy, and had no connection whatsoever to the state of her personal life—which happened to be in crisis.

Groaning, she lifted her head slightly and spotted the tin waste basket beside the desk. It would do if in a pinch she failed to reach the bathroom in time.

Several minutes and two dry crackers later, the nausea receded. Sips from her water bottle also helped. Eventually, she resumed studying the schedule, though she still found it hard to concentrate.

Four hundred fewer steers were going to make a difference in the workload and reduce the burden her half-day schedule had put on Cole and the ranch hands.

Then again, that might change when he left. She'd heard about Gabe and Josh offering to buy his share of the ranch with proceeds from the sale. The remaining funds had been deposited yesterday, and the transport trucks arrived bright and early. Josh had overseen the loading of the steers. Violet stopped by to watch but hadn't stayed.

When the family didn't get together last night for a big dinner, Violet assumed Cole had accepted his brothers' offer. That only made sense. Without money from the sale to pay off the remainder of August's medical bills, there had been no reason to celebrate.

Gabe and Raquel wanted Cole to stay. They hadn't said it out loud, but she could tell they'd come to love him. She thought Cole might love them, too, and was just as tight-lipped.

A sharp knock caused her to glance up. Cara stood in the open doorway.

"Am I interrupting?"

"Not at all." Violet motioned to her friend and sat up straighter, pushing the schedule aside. "I'm pretty much done."

"I saw your truck parked outside and wanted to see how you're doing. Raquel mentioned you've been looking pale lately."

There was no chair for Cara to sit on. Brushing a thick layer of dust off an old wooden box, she delicately lowered herself onto it.

"Morning sickness," Violet complained. "Even in the middle of the afternoon. It comes and goes."

"Anything I can do to help?"

Violet shook her head. "I'll be fine."

"Well, let me know."

"Hey, congratulations on your engagement, by the way. I haven't had a chance to tell you."

"Thanks." Cara's entire face lit up.

"You must be excited."

"I never dreamed I'd get married again. Just goes to show you how things can change."

Violet couldn't agree more. Here she was, fourteen weeks pregnant. Who'd have guessed? And who'd have guessed her baby's father would be leaving soon without her lifting a finger to stop him.

Should she? Did she even want to? Why hadn't he told her in person? He owed her that much.

Cara jumped to her feet and held out her hand, showing off her new ring. Violet rose slowly, careful of her unpredictable stomach, and leaned in for a closer inspection.

"It's beautiful."

"I love it," Cara admitted, on the verge of tears. "We picked it out together. You don't think that's unromantic, do you? Shopping for a ring together?"

"It's wonderfully romantic." Violet pulled her friend close for a quick hug. "Have you picked a date yet?"

"August twenty-fifth."

"So soon!"

"Why wait?" A rosy glow colored Cara's cheeks.

Why indeed? "I'm really happy for you," Violet said. "And I expect to be included in all the wedding activities. Shower. Dress buying. Reception planning."

"Well, since you brought it up, I'd really like for you to be one of my bridesmaids."

A knot of pain instantly formed in Violet's chest. Cole would no doubt be in the wedding party, too, as Josh's best man. Could she handle it?

She'd have to find a way. There was no other choice.

Hugging Cara again, she said, "I'd love to be your bridesmaid. As long as you don't mind my big belly showing."

"Are you kidding? I'm thrilled about your belly."

"Me, too."

The knot of pain doubled in size, and Violet fought for control. Her emotions were getting the best of her today. She was delighted for Cara. She was also a tiny bit jealous. Had things gone differently with Cole, she might be getting married, too, and asking Cara to be her bridesmaid.

"You're going to be a wonderful mother." Cara suddenly became emotional and blinked quickly, as if she might cry. A moment later, her eyes misted.

Violet drew back to gaze at her. "Are you okay?"

"I haven't told anyone." Cara sniffed. "Swear you won't say a word until Josh and I are ready. I don't want…in case…"

Violet gasped. All at once, she knew. "You're pregnant!"

"Not even a month along. I took the home pregnancy test yesterday and I go to the doctor on Tuesday."

"Oh, Cara." Violet was truly pleased for her friend.

"I wasn't sure after Javier died if I could bear having another child." Her smile was both infectious and heart wrenching. "I haven't been this happy in years."

"No guilt. You're entitled to all the happiness you can find."

"You, too, you know."

Violet shrugged. "I guess it wasn't in the cards. I mean, I am happy. About the baby." Her own tears threatened to fall. "It's different this time. I'm going to carry to term. I swear I can almost feel the baby growing inside me."

"Of course you will. And your baby will be gorgeous."

Would he or she look like Cole, with his incredible blue eyes?

Violet tried to smile. Her mouth, however, refused to cooperate.

"What happened between you and Cole, if you don't mind me asking?" Cara's eyes filled with sympathy. "Did it have to do with your parents?"

"Yes, and his mom. But there's more to it than that. The debacle at dinner…it brought out our worst insecurities, and we let them derail us."

"I'm sorry."

"Yeah, well, if our relationship had been strong enough to start with, he wouldn't have been scared off so easily."

"Please don't take this the wrong way, but I think it's more than insecurities."

"What?" Violet's interest was genuine. She'd had only her own opinions to mull over this past week.

"Come on." Cara nodded toward the door. "We need some fresh air and sunshine. This place is stuffy."

Leaving the dusty, dreary shed, they walked toward the stalls where the therapy horses resided. During their stroll, Violet recounted the details of her and Cole's disagreement, trying not to lay the blame at his feet, but fearing she had.

"Can you understand how he feels?" Cara asked. "Much as we loved August, he set a horrible example for Cole and Josh. Their mother, too." She rolled her eyes. "I still can't believe how selfish she is."

"She was hurt badly by August," Violet said. "He had a child with another woman while they were still married."

"That doesn't give her the right to prejudice her sons against him."

"No?"

"You're not supporting Miranda?" Cara looked aghast.

"August was wonderful to me. I'll be forever grateful to him. But he was also a first-class jerk to his wife and children. All his children. What he did wasn't fair." She hadn't realized that until Cole showed her a side of August she hadn't known. "He should have divorced Miranda before taking up with Raquel. And he should have fought harder to maintain a relationship with Cole and Josh. Their anger at him is justified. It's the reason Cole's afraid of making a commitment."

Violet paused and drew in a breath, her short speech draining her. If only she'd made it up to Cole when she had the chance. If only she'd listened to him instead of constantly defending August. Cole might not be leaving now.

She and Cara stopped in front of a stall and Cara patted a gentle mare called Mama. The horse was one of several examples of how much Cole was needed here.

"I should have been more patient with him," Violet admitted. "Except patience isn't my strong suit."

"Don't give up, Violet." Cara spoke with vehemence. "If you do, you'll be right back where you started. Having a baby alone isn't what you want, I don't care what you say. You love Cole, and he loves you."

"Not enough."

Violet had been blind before. She'd refused to see that until Cole let go of his anger at his father, he was incapable of forming a healthy and loving relationship with her or with anyone.

"August tried to make amends in the end," Cara said in a mournful voice. "That counts for something."

"It does. He reunited Gabe and Josh. And to a lesser degree, Gabe and Cole."

Cara faced Violet, a change in her expression. "Have you talked to him lately?"

"No." Violet mustered her courage. "How is he?"

"You should ask him yourself."

"When's he leaving?"

"Violet," Cara said earnestly, "he's not."

"No?"

"What made you think that?"

Violet couldn't answer right away. The shock had yet to wear off. "His brothers paid him for his share of the ranch. Raquel told me."

"He didn't take their offer."

"Why?"

Cara stared at her in astonishment. "I'd think you'd be glad."

"I...am."

"Then go talk to him. He's in section four. A few of the young steers escaped the roundup. He's locating them now."

Violet didn't move.

"What's wrong?"

"I don't know."

"Violet." Cara took her by both shoulders. "There's only one reason he refused the offer. You."

"He feels responsible for the baby."

"He does. But he wouldn't have to stay to be a responsible father."

"What do I say to him?"

"You'll think of something on the way."

When Violet still didn't move, Cara gave her a nudge. "Go on. Get out of here."

"But I—"

"You have nothing to lose. More importantly, you have a lot to gain."

She did. Except the last time she'd crawled out on that limb for Cole, she'd fallen off and was still smarting from the hard landing.

"I'm scared," she admitted.

"Don't let that stop you. You'll regret it for the rest of

your life, trust me. I spent too many years playing the
what-if game, and it got me nothing but misery. When I
finally stopped, my whole life changed."

She made it sound easy. "What if he says no?"

Cara grinned. "What if he says yes?"

Could she be right? Had Cole turned down his brothers because he wanted to give the two of them a second
chance? There was only one way to find out.

Saying goodbye to Cara, Violet hurried to her truck.
At the gate leading to the pastures, she turned southwest.
Section four lay a mile and a half ahead.

As she drove the narrow and bumpy road, she couldn't
shake the sensation she was driving straight into her future, one that included Cole.

"MOVE ALONG, SLOWPOKE." Cole herded the final reluctant
steer toward the livestock trailer.

At the last second, it cut to the right and tried to run. In
a flash, Hotshot pivoted, blocking the steer and leaving it
no choice but to clamber into the trailer as the four others
before him had done.

Dismounting, Cole held the reins in one hand and
slammed the trailer door with his other. "We're good to
go," he hollered to Joey, and secured the latch.

The ornery steer bellowed and kicked in protest, making a loud racket. He disliked being forced to ride in an
enclosed vehicle, even if it would deliver him to the herd
grazing two sections over.

Joey hung his left arm and his head out the driver's side
window. "Meet you back at the ranch," he said, and waved.

Cole watched the truck and trailer pull forward, reluctant to mount Hotshot and ride home. He preferred
the solitude of these wide-open spaces after the past few
tension-filled weeks.

Between his mother and Vi's parents and all the dissension they'd wreaked; his disagreement with Vi; the arrival of the transport vehicles and the departure of the purchased steers, not to mention the pressure from his brothers to accept or decline their offer, he was tired. More tired than he could ever remember being.

"Let's go home, boy."

Tossing the reins over Hotshot's neck, he put his boot in the stirrup and swung easily up into the saddle. It was his favorite, the one he'd used most for rodeoing, and it fit him well. Like his hat, the saddle had seen him through many a time, both good and bad. With luck, it would see him through this next phase of his life.

Hotshot needed no directing. Lowering his head, he automatically started toward the ranch at an easy pace.

Cole commended himself yet again for choosing this horse from among hundreds. The gelding had made incredible progress. The same could also be said about the pony Cole was training for Blake Nolan.

During Blake's visit with his kids the day before, he'd complimented Cole on the pony's great strides in such a short time. He'd promised to spread the word and for Cole to expect new clients, along with a bonus. Already Cole had received one referral and been ridiculously pleased.

Vi, it seemed, was right. Cole had options other than rodeoing and returning to California. He'd simply been too stubborn to see.

Speaking of stubborn, he should have called her, if only to check on her health. Instead, he'd relied on getting news of her secondhand from Raquel, who couldn't hide her displeasure when she'd reported that Vi's morning sickness had returned.

She wanted Cole to reconcile with Vi. He wanted it, too. At least, he wanted theirs to be an amicable relationship. How could they successfully parent their child if they didn't get along? Except he was clueless when it came to patching up their differences, having never done it before, and having no example in his family to follow. The Dempseys didn't mend bridges. Rather, they let them burn to the ground.

There were also all Vi's quick turns in the opposite direction and obvious attempts at avoiding him to consider. He might want to attempt a reconciliation, but she obviously didn't. He fully expected her to slam the door in his face if he attempted to see her.

Give her more time, he told himself. She hadn't had much of an example to follow, either, between her parents and her marriage to Denny.

Waiting would be hard, however. Cole needed Vi. Was lost without her. Looking back, he realized theirs had been the kind of relationship he'd thought wasn't possible. One he'd made impossible by royally screwing up. He should have shown her how much she meant to him. Got down on his knees like Josh had said. Instead, he'd walked away.

Letting his thoughts drift, he listened to the rhythmic clip-clop of Hotshot's hoofs. It suddenly occurred to him how much he'd come to enjoy life on a cattle ranch. With the remainder of his dad's medical bills soon to be paid off, he might actually be able to carve out a decent living. Especially with the occasional horse-training client. He might even talk to the Powells about those roping clinics.

What would his father say to hear that Cole liked ranching and had decided to stay on? The old man was probably right now having himself a good laugh, if such a thing were possible in the afterlife.

Raising his arm, Cole shaded his eyes from the blistering sun and squinted into the distance. Was that a truck on the rise? As he watched, the speck grew steadily larger.

He jerked back on the reins. Were his eyes playing tricks on him? Could that possibly be Vi's pickup?

His heart jammed to a halt before starting up again in triple time. It *was* Vi's truck! What was she doing, driving all the way out here?

He cautioned himself to remain calm and waited in the middle of the road, Hotshot bobbing his head. She stopped about ten feet in front of him. The next moment, the door opened and she emerged. Standing there, she looked straight at him. Surprise, surprise, no averting her eyes or ducking behind corners.

"Hi," she said.

Cole stayed in the saddle. "If you're here to check on me—"

"I'm not."

"Really."

"No need. I'm sure the stray steers have been rounded up."

"For the record, they have."

"You're doing a good job, Cole. I should have told you that before."

He nodded, her praise meaning more to him than he cared to admit. "Thanks."

"I'm glad, because it looks like I'm going to continue at half days for the rest of my pregnancy. I'll also be taking off a few months when the baby's born. Dos Estrellas is going to need a dependable and competent livestock manager to cover for me."

"You don't have to worry, Vi. I'm not leaving."

"That's what I heard. And I'm not worried. You're a fine rancher, Cole. But then, you come by it honestly."

He climbed off Hotshot, uncertain about his next move until he saw the flash of hope in her eyes. Dropping the reins, he strode toward her. Hotshot meandered off, going only so far as the closest clump of grass.

"I'm curious." She studied him intently. "You're giving up the things you've wanted since you got here. Money and your freedom. I'd like to know why. I think I'm entitled."

God, was he really once that callous and shallow? "Don't forget sticking it to my late father and Gabe. That was highest on my list."

A tiny glint of humor lit her features. "What's important is that you didn't stick it to them."

Emotions warred inside him, and he wondered if he'd ever find peace. "I still think my dad was wrong. He made a lot of bad decisions. When he had the chance to rectify them, he chose not to. That's hard to forgive."

"I understand."

"But I can and will put it behind me, Vi." He smiled, though he still felt sad. "I'm tired of anger and resentment directing the course of my life. I'm ready for a change. To quit being like my mom. I didn't realize how much I resembled her until last week. It was a rude awakening, let me tell you."

Vi tilted her head at an appealing angle. "I know I've said this before, but you're far more like your dad. He was confident in himself, whether or not he was right."

"I'm right in this case. My future is in Mustang Valley."

"That makes me happy."

He wished he could be sure. He was anything but confident when it came to Vi's feelings for him.

"I have a new client." He hadn't told anyone yet.

"You do?" She beamed.

"The De Marcoses. Blake Nolan recommended me to them, if you can believe it."

"I know them." She gave him a curious look. "They have small children."

"Right." He grinned wryly. "It appears I'm gaining a reputation in the area as a trainer of kids' horses. Not exactly what I envisioned for myself."

"I'm sorry," she said, laughing behind her hand. "It's not funny."

"It is. I'd laugh, too, if not for the money."

"I'm glad you aren't limiting yourself."

He sobered. "I'll do it, Vi. I'll support our child and be there for him or her. Always. I'm going to be a better father than my dad was."

"I can't ask for more."

"Yes, you can. You should." He shortened the distance between them. "I promise you I'm going to work my tail off to be worthy of our child and you. I was wrong the other day. And if you kick me to the curb, I wouldn't blame you. I'd hate it, but I'd—"

He didn't finish because she came to him then, ending his torture. He held her tight, hoping she sensed the depth of his love.

"I'm sorry, Vi. For everything."

"I'm the one who should be apologizing. The way I talked to you, I'm no better than my parents. I guess the apple doesn't fall far from the tree."

He hoisted her up onto her toes, reveling in the contact of her soft body and how exquisitely she fit against him. "It does fall very far. We're proof of that."

"I wouldn't want anyone else for the father of my baby."

Nothing had ever touched him more. "Be careful. That almost sounds like you love me."

"I—"

He brought his mouth close to hers, stopping her before she could finish. "Let me be the first to say it. I love you. On some level, I think I knew the second I walked into the bar that night I'd met the woman I was meant to spend the rest of my life with."

"I'm glad you feel that way, because we're really going to have this baby."

"I can't wait."

She pulled back in order to search his face. What she saw must have satisfied her. "I love you, too, Cole. I didn't think it was possible. These past few months have been incredible."

"Speaking of incredible..." He kissed her then, since holding her had ceased to be enough.

At the touch of her lips on his, everything that was wrong became instantly right. Every mistake, every regret forgotten.

"Are you free tonight?" he asked, when they broke apart, his mouth poised close to hers. "I could cook dinner. We can talk."

"I thought you couldn't cook."

"I didn't say it would be good."

"I'm not busy," she said shyly. "But let's eat at my house. So we can be alone.

He kissed her again. How could he not? When she returned his passion in equal measure, he began to believe in a future he'd always thought beyond his reach.

Eventually, he had to let her go, but he fully intended on resuming later tonight.

"I'm going to court you, Vi," he said. "The way I should have from the start. And after a while, not long, mind you, I'm going to ask you to marry me. I think a week should do it. Two at the most."

"And I'm going to accept, Cole Dempsey." Her smile outshone the sun. "Just so you know."

"Good. Otherwise, I'd have to pester you until you came to your senses."

They tied Hotshot to the back of her truck and very slowly drove home, both to accommodate the horse and because they didn't want their time together to end.

Cole couldn't help thinking that he'd come full circle. Only by returning to Dos Estrellas, the place where his life had started, was he able to find everything he needed to complete it. Home, happiness, a family and the love of his life.

* * * * *

Watch for the next book in
Cathy McDavid's MUSTANG VALLEY *miniseries,*
RESCUING THE COWBOY,
available October 2016.

REQUEST YOUR FREE BOOKS!
2 FREE NOVELS PLUS 2 FREE GIFTS!

⊞ HARLEQUIN®

American Romance®

LOVE, HOME & HAPPINESS

"Welcome aboard!" The flight attendant smiled. "Going home to Texas…?"

"Not voluntarily," Garrett Lockhart muttered under his breath.

It wasn't that he didn't *appreciate* spending time with his family. He did. It's just that he didn't want them weighing in on what his next step should be.

Reenlist and take the considerable promotion being offered?

Or take a civilian post that would allow him to pursue his dreams?

He had twenty-nine days to decide and an unspecified but pressing family crisis to handle in the meantime.

And an expensive-looking blonde in a white power suit who'd been sizing him up from a distance, ever since he arrived at the gate…

He'd noticed her, too. Hard not to with that gorgeous face, mane of long, silky hair brushing against her shoulders, and a smoking-hot body.

Phone to her ear, one hand trying to retract the telescoping handle of her suitcase while still managing the carryall over her shoulder, she said, "Have to go…Yes, yes. I'll call you as soon as I land in Dallas. Not to worry." She laughed softly, charmingly, while lifting her suitcase with one hand into the overhead compartment. "If you-all will just *wait* until I can—*ouch*!" He heard her stumble toward him, yelping as her expensive leather carryall crashed onto his lap.

"Let me help you," he drawled. With one hand hooked around her waist and the other around her shoulders, he lifted her quickly and skillfully to her feet, then turned and lowered her so she landed squarely in her own seat. That done, he handed her the carryall she'd inadvertently assaulted him with.

Hope knew she should say something. If only to make her later job easier.

And she would have, if the sea blue eyes she'd been staring into hadn't been so mesmerizing. She liked his hair, too. So dark and thick and…touchable…

"Ma'am?" he prodded again, less patiently.

Clearly he was expecting some response to ease the unabashed sexual tension that had sprung up between them, so she said the first thing that came into her mind. "Thank you for your assistance just now. And for your service. To our country, I mean."

His dark brow furrowed. His lips—so firm and sensual—thinned. Shoulders flexing, he studied her with breathtaking intent, then asked, "How'd you know I was in the military?"

Don't miss
A TEXAS SOLDIER'S FAMILY
by Cathy Gillen Thacker, available July 2016
everywhere Harlequin® Western Romance®
books and ebooks are sold.

www.Harlequin.com

Same great stories, new name!

In July 2016,
the HARLEQUIN®
AMERICAN ROMANCE® series
will become
the HARLEQUIN®
WESTERN ROMANCE series.

Connect with us to find your next great read,
special offers and more.

f /HarlequinBooks

🐦 @HarlequinBooks

www.HarlequinBlog.com

www.Harlequin.com/Newsletters

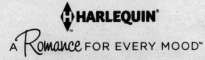

A *Romance* FOR EVERY MOOD™

www.Harlequin.com

HWR2016

Turn your love of reading into rewards you'll love with
Harlequin My Rewards

**Join for FREE today at
www.HarlequinMyRewards.com**

Earn **FREE BOOKS** of your choice.

Experience **EXCLUSIVE OFFERS** and contests.

Enjoy **BOOK RECOMMENDATIONS**
selected just for you.

PLUS! Sign up now
and get **500** points
right away!

MYR16R